ELLA AT EDEN

D1020986

For Danielle, Yvette and Meredith—the village raising Ella.

First American Edition 2021
Kane Miller, A Division of EDC Publishing

Text copyright © Laura Sieveking, 2020.
Cover and internal illustrations copyright © Scholastic Australia, 2020.
Cover and internal illustrations by Danielle McDonald.
Design by Keisha Galbraith.
Laura Sieveking asserts her moral rights as the author of this work.
Danielle McDonald asserts her moral rights as the illustrator of this work.

First published by Scholastic Australia, an imprint of Scholastic Australia Pty Limited.
This edition published under license from Scholastic Australia Pty Limited.

For information contact:
Kane Miller, A Division of EDC Publishing
5402 S. 122nd E. Ave, Tulsa, OK 74146
www.kanemiller.com
www.myubam.com

Library of Congress Control Number: 2021930858

Printed and bound in the United States of America

1 2 3 4 5 6 7 8 9 10

ISBN: 978-1-68464-357-8

ELLA AT EDEN

New Girl

LAURA SIEVEKING

Kane Miller
A DIVISION OF EDC PUBLISHING

Eden College

Multipurpose fields/courts

Field

Sick bay

Sports & aquatic center

Office

Juniors' dorm

Centenary Lawn

Dining hall

Bell tower

Main building (classrooms/ science labs)

Fountain

Central courtyard

Main gate

Seniors' dorm

Music, art & drama center

Auditorium

Teacher accommodation

Library

Function hall

4

Juniors' Dorm

Level 2   Year 7 rooms

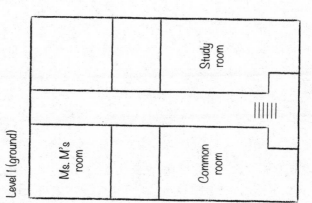

	Bathroom	
6		7
5		8
4 Ella's room		9
3		10
2		11
1	‖‖‖‖‖	12

Level 1 (ground)

Ms. M's room		
		Study room
Common room	‖‖‖‖‖	

5

Chapter 1

I looked up at the stone tower which disappeared into the clear blue sky. I squeezed Olivia's hand. She looked back at me with her deep brown eyes and raised her eyebrows. It was almost like she was silently saying, *It's not too late to back out!*

My tummy fluttered with nerves and I noticed my breaths were quick and shallow. I felt Mum's reassuring hand on my shoulder. My breathing calmed.

My little brother, Max, was jumping off a low stone wall, striking the air with a karate kick each time. He didn't seem to appreciate what was going on.

That today was a day of big change for our family. Dad waved at him to get off the wall and come and join the rest of us. I saw Max's mouth utter the words, "Aw, man!"

I smiled.

The courtyard we were standing in was vast—it looked as big as my entire primary school! All around the perimeter of the immaculately paved courtyard were various old buildings glinting in the sunlight. Big, sandstone buildings with pointy tops. All that was missing was a princess trailing her hair out a top window.

A loudspeaker let out a little squeal as it came to life. A voice boomed into the air. "Everyone, please gather around the fountain."

We shuffled over to the fountain in the middle of the courtyard.

"It is now time to bid farewell to your families," the voice said. Suddenly, everything hit me all at once. What was I doing here? Had I really agreed to this? Was I really going to *live* here, without my family? I looked up at Mum and searched her face. Maybe she thought this was a bad idea—maybe we should just go home.

Mum's eyes were glistening. "I'm so proud of you, Ella," she sniffed.

"Me too, possum," Dad said, putting out his hand to ruffle my hair. "I know you'll do your best." I instinctively jumped back—I'd spent ages getting my hair just right for my first day. I'd pulled back my long, thick, brown hair into a high ponytail this morning and secured it with a white ribbon. I'd read in the Student Handbook that you have to wear a ribbon at this school. Now, don't get me wrong, I love accessorizing as much as the next girl, but the rules of this place said we *had* to wear a *white* ribbon. I remember standing in the uniform shop over the summer and complaining to the lady who worked there. "How am I going to express myself with a plain white ribbon?!" The lady thought that was really funny, but I have no idea why.

I straightened my royal-blue blazer. It felt odd to be wearing a school uniform on a Saturday. But Saturday was the day all the new Year 7 girls had to start school.

Max tugged my blazer sleeve. His eyes were suddenly filled with worry. It was like he'd finally worked out why we were here. "I'm really going to miss you, Ella," he said in a small voice.

"Oh, Max," I said, pulling my little brother into a big hug. I wasn't going to miss Max's snail collection. Or his messy room. Or his stinky axolotl tank. But I would miss *him*.

"And you," I said, turning to my little sister. "I'd better not come home at Christmas to find you've taken over my room!"

Olivia didn't laugh. She just nodded sadly.

"Come here," I said, grabbing her arm and hugging her tight.

"Don't go," Olivia whispered.

"I'll miss you, too," I whispered back.

Mum and Dad hugged me close. I could tell Mum was putting on a brave face, holding back tears. But Dad's eyes shone with pride. As they released me, Mum straightened my uniform.

"Now, would all students please gather together,

and all families please depart by the main gate. Thank you for being here today to support your girls as they start their new adventure," the voice said over the loudspeaker.

I looked around and saw lots of girls with teary, red eyes. Some were clinging to their parents, but others were bouncing up and down with excitement.

Next to my family, I could see my best friend, Zoe, hugging her parents. Her teenage brother stood awkwardly beside them, but after her parents released her, he also pulled her into a big hug. She gave a final wave to her parents, who joined my family as they walked toward the main gate together.

I linked arms with my best friend, and we shuffled over to the collection of students in the middle of the courtyard. We turned to watch as the families slowly walked through the giant gate at the entrance to the school. I gave a final wave as my entire family disappeared out of view.

Deep breath.

"Gather around," the voice said. Now we could see

who was speaking. It was an older woman with a warm face and small, round glasses perched on the end of her nose. She had a welcoming smile and reminded me of my Nanna Kate. But maybe a bit younger. I knew immediately who it was: Mrs. Sinclair, the school Headmistress. I'd had an interview with her last year when I was applying to the school.

"Welcome, welcome," she gushed. "Welcome to Eden College!"

The girls around me released a collective gasp—it was a mix of excitement and nerves. We were finally here! I couldn't quite believe it myself. I was an Eden Girl!

Suddenly, all my nerves melted away and I remembered why I wanted to be an Eden Girl in the first place.

It started last year.

Zoe had told me at the beginning of Year 6 that she was going to Eden College for high school the next year. She thought I'd be mad, but I was just sad. Everyone knows that Eden College is a prestigious boarding school for girls, which means all the girls live at the school. *Prestigious* is a word I like to use in my writing. It means special or fancy or highly regarded. To be honest, I was a little jealous that Zoe was going to Eden. I'd heard all about the amazing buildings, the fabulous teachers and all the incredible opportunities there. Like, Eden has an award-winning orchestra (which seemed totally unfair because Zoe doesn't play an instrument anymore and I play the flute). It also has a gymnastics program, drama club, musical society, dance troupe and debate team. These are all things I like to do, but hardly any of them are offered at my local high school.

I asked Mum if I could apply to Eden College, but she said it was too expensive. I was forlorn. That means pitifully sad. Not only was I missing out on all these incredible things, but I was losing my best friend at the same time.

Then one day, about halfway through last year, Mum and Dad came into my room and sat on my bed. I knew that meant we were about to have one of our Very

Serious Conversations (or VSCs, as Olivia and I call them). These only happen when big things are going on, like when our parents tell us we are moving or getting a new baby brother or that Great-Nanna Peggy is really sick. So, Mum and Dad closed my bedroom door behind them and sat on my bed with their VSC faces on. Mum had a pile of brochures in her hand and I wondered for a split second if they were selling the house and moving us to Abu Dhabi like my friend Nadine's parents did.

But it wasn't about Abu Dhabi.

Mum spread the brochures out on the bed and they were all about Eden College. I looked at her with a confused face because she'd already told me that I couldn't be an Eden Girl. But that's when she showed me a brochure titled *Scholarships*. Scholarships are special places awarded to students who are really good at different things. And they get to go to the school for free. There were academic scholarships, music scholarships and sports scholarships. But Dad pointed to one called the All-Rounder Scholarship. This made no sense to me, so he explained it's for a girl

14

who likes to do all sorts of things. A girl who is good at schoolwork, but also loves to get involved in activities like sports, music, drama and other things which "enrich the school," as the brochure said. I admitted I was doing pretty well at school, especially in writing. And I play the flute and do gymnastics and ballet. And just that year I'd learned to debate, which is a fancy word for organized arguing (and I happen to be *really* good at that, too). So maybe I *could* get the All-Rounder Scholarship?

The next few months were full of tests and interviews. I had to go to Eden College with my parents and meet the headmistress and tell her how much I would like to be an Eden Girl.

Then we waited.

We waited for what seemed like an eternity. But finally, one spring day, I got a letter in the mail. It was addressed to me and had the Eden College crest on the front. I gently opened the crisp, white envelope and read the letter inside.

I was in!

"As you all know from your interviews, I am the Headmistress, Mrs. Sinclair," Mrs. Sinclair said, her voice snapping me back to the present. "And this is the Year 7 Coordinator and your Housemistress, Ms. Montgomery. She is also the Vice Headmistress of the school."

Mrs. Sinclair gestured to her left where a tall, thin woman stood. She had a narrow face and dark eyebrows which pointed upward like sharp arrows. She wore black pants with a matching blazer, a white business shirt and what my Nanna Kate would describe as "sensible" shoes.

"Welcome," she said in a cool voice. "As your Housemistress, it is my job to look after you all in the dormitory. I trust you will quickly grasp the rules of Eden College. Part of being an Eden Girl is learning to be respectful, and that is something I demand from all the girls under my care."

Zoe raised her eyebrows at me.

"Yes, indeed, respect is important," Mrs. Sinclair said with a smile. "But we also want our girls to feel empowered, supported and valued."

Ms. Montgomery took a sharp, audible breath and glanced upward. She seemed annoyed.

"So, if you would please follow me," Mrs. Sinclair continued, "I will show you to the dormitory. This is where you will live while you are here at school. It will be your home away from home. I do hope you like it."

All the girls in the group nervously shuffled forward, following Mrs. Sinclair and Ms. Montgomery as they led us through the courtyard. We passed more of the old-fashioned sandstone buildings with their pointy tops and majestic columns. The path we were walking on was swept clean, and beautifully manicured gardens hugged the edges.

"To your right, you will see the sports and aquatic center," Mrs. Sinclair said, pointing to a more modern-looking building. I peeked through one of the fogged-up windows and could see a massive swimming pool with lane ropes, starting blocks and diving boards.

"And over there to your left is the music and drama center," Mrs. Sinclair said, pointing.

My heart started to beat just a little faster. Music and drama were subjects that I adored and I couldn't wait to see what we would be doing in that building.

We passed the main building, which housed the classrooms, and emerged onto an expansive green lawn. The lawn was rimmed with beautiful gardens of roses and there was an abstract metal statue in the center. Beyond the lawn we could see a gorgeous set of houses.

"And down here are the dorms," Mrs. Sinclair said with a gushing sigh, and led us toward a building to our right.

It looked like a cottage with its pointed, red-brick roof, but it was much, much bigger than any cottage I had ever stayed in. There were at least three stories, maybe four. And it was stunning.

We walked into the foyer of the house and saw a large, cascading staircase with a dark-brown, shiny banister. If Olivia was here she would have raced up the stairs and whooshed down the banister on her bottom, probably falling over at the end. That girl has no sense of propriety (that means having good manners and being all proper).

It was at that point Mrs. Sinclair said she was going to leave us in the "capable hands" of Ms. Montgomery. I thought her hands looked more cold and bony than capable.

"The Year 7 rooms are on the second floor and there are four girls to a room. Years 8 and 9 are on the third floor and our senior girls in Years 10 to 12 are in a different building. On this first floor, past the stairs on your right, is the study room. And down here on your left," Ms. Montgomery said, as she gestured through the foyer and down the hallway, "is the common room. This is the student lounge where you are able to spend leisure time with your classmates."

We walked into the huge room which had couches, beanbags, cushions and a large TV mounted on the wall.

"I see you all eyeing the television," Ms. Montgomery said, disapprovingly. "I'll have you know, television is only to be viewed during set hours and once all homework is done."

The place was empty except for our Year 7 group.

All the other years were returning to school tomorrow. Mrs. Sinclair had said this was so we could settle in quietly without the house being too full.

I began to wonder who was going to be in my room.

As if reading my mind, Ms. Montgomery told us all to find a place to sit. "I am now going to sort you into your dormitory rooms."

Chapter 2

Sort us into our rooms? My nerves came flooding back. These were the girls I was going to be living in a room with for the whole year. What if I was with someone mean? What if my roommates snored?

From the sideboard, Ms. Montgomery picked up a piece of paper with lists of names on it.

She read through the dorm room names—well, actually, they were just numbers which was a bit boring—as well as the names of the girls in each room. I so desperately wanted to be with Zoe. We clutched each other's hands hopefully.

"Dormitory room four: Zoe, Grace, Ella and Violet."

I squealed and hugged Zoe.

"That will be quite enough!" Ms. Montgomery barked. "Please go up to your room *quietly.*"

I quickly let go of Zoe and squashed down my excitement. I straightened my blazer and clasped my panama hat as we began to walk up the wide staircase to the second floor. The hallway was carpeted with warm, plush, cream carpet, and along the walls hung paintings of former headmistresses of the school.

"It's like they're watching us," Zoe giggled, as she gazed at each stern face looking down on us from the wall.

"Look at this one," I blurted. "Ms. Antoinette Bellavance, Headmistress, 1945–1951," I read in a posh voice from the plaque below the painting. "She looks like an old dinosaur!"

Zoe burst out laughing.

"Um, excuse me! What did you just say?" a terse voice said from behind me.

I turned to see a tall girl, frowning intensely. She had a high ponytail with thick, blond hair which flowed over her shoulders like a mane.

"Sorry?" I asked, confused.

"What did you just say?" she barked.

"Oh, we were just having a bit of a joke about this hallway of old dinosaurs," I said lightly, trying to make her laugh.

"That 'old dinosaur' is my great-grandmother!" the girl yelled.

Zoe coughed loudly to smother her giggles.

"Oh, I'm so sorry!" I bumbled. "I didn't mean to be rude. I mean, she looks like a really . . . nice person. I'm sure she was a great headmistress . . ." The words spilled out of my mouth so quickly I barely knew what I was actually saying.

"What's going on here? Why are you dawdling in the hallway?" Ms. Montgomery's voice floated up the stairs. She glided up the corridor and stopped right in front of us. "Saskia, what's the problem?"

The tall, blond girl, obviously named Saskia, stabbed

her finger in my direction. "*This* girl thinks it's funny to make fun of our founding headmistresses," she hissed. "Including *my* great-grandmother!"

"What is your name?" Ms. Montgomery asked, narrowing her eyes at me.

"E . . . Ella," I stammered.

"Well, Ella. I want you to know that we do not tolerate disrespect at Eden College! Now, apologize to Saskia."

"Sorry, Saskia," I mumbled.

"Sorry, Saskia," Zoe echoed.

"I'll be keeping an eye on you," Ms. Montgomery said, as she marched off down the hall.

Saskia raised one eyebrow at me, then, with a flick of her ponytail, stalked off.

"That's just great," I moaned. "Day one and the housemistress already knows my name, for all the wrong reasons!"

"Don't worry, Ella," Zoe said, linking her arm with mine. "There's plenty of time to make a good impression. I'm sure that girl Saskia will have forgotten all about this by tomorrow."

But I had a feeling that Saskia wasn't the type to quickly forgive and forget.

"Come on," Zoe said, pulling me gently down the hall. "Let's find our room."

We walked past bedrooms one, two and three and stopped outside a door with a gold number four on it. I pushed it open and we stepped inside. The room was large and bright. No purple walls, much to my disappointment, but it did look very clean. There were four single beds—two on one wall and two on the other. Along the back wall was a large bay window. It had a real, built-in window seat, with soft, plump cushions to sit on. The sun shone through the window, warming the room. Everything in me wanted to leap onto the cushions with my writing journal or a good book and just sit there in my own little world.

"Cool," Zoe whispered.

Sitting on one of the beds was a girl I hadn't seen before. She must have made her way into our dorm room while we were in the hallway with Saskia.

She looked up at us with bright green eyes that shone against her olive skin. Her dark hair was neatly braided with a white ribbon at the bottom.

"Hi," she chirped. "I'm Grace. I hope you don't mind that I chose a bed already. I mean, I can totally move if you guys want this bed, but if you're happy with me here then that works too! Your bags are already here against the wall. They brought them up to our rooms for us, how cool is that? I've heard you're allowed to decorate around your bed with stuff from home. This window's pretty nice, isn't it?"

Zoe and I stared with wide eyes. I'd never heard someone speak so fast.

"Sorry, my mum warned me not to be such a chatterbox. She said I might scare people off a bit, so I should just 'chill out.' But once I start talking, it's hard to stop, you know? What are your names?"

"I'm Ella," I laughed. "And this is my best friend, Zoe. We went to the same primary school."

"Oh, you are so lucky!" Grace gasped. "I don't know anyone here. I've been so nervous about who will be in my room, but you two look nice!"

Zoe giggled.

"Excuse me, can I please get through?" a small voice said behind us.

"And you must be our number four!" Grace said, jumping off the bed to welcome the fourth member of our dorm. "I'm Grace, this is Ella and that's Chloe . . ."

"Ah, it's Zoe," Zoe corrected.

"Oops! Sorry, Zoe!" Grace said, hitting herself on the forehead. "I'm terrible with names! Mum says that's because I'm always talking and never listening properly—can you believe that? How rude! What's your name, number four?"

The newest member of our room slowly looked up at us from behind her round glasses. She was a tiny little thing—probably only the size of Olivia, who is two whole years younger than me. Her skin was pale and her eyes were deep brown.

"I'm Violet," she whispered.

"Hi, Violet! Do you like Violet or Vi? I have an aunt called Violet. She's horrible. But you look nice!"

Grace's words tumbled out of her mouth.

"Just Violet," our new roommate said in a flat voice. She walked over to her bag and pulled it to a bed. Without looking at us, she began to unpack her things, quietly sorting them into piles.

Now, my Nanna Kate says "never judge a book by its cover." I always thought this was a bit of a silly thing to say—of *course* I'm going to judge a book by its cover. If the cover is full of sharks, like Max's *Great Guide to the World of Sharks*, then there's no way I'm going to touch that book. But Nanna Kate says what she really means is not to assume you know all about someone just from your first meeting. I wasn't sure what was up with this Violet character, but she was either super shy or super unfriendly.

I guess we'd find out pretty soon, considering she was going to be living in our room.

Chapter 3

× −

From: <u>Ella</u>

Sent: Saturday, 5:40 PM

To: <u>Olivia</u>

Subject: Day one done!

Hi Olivia!

Do you miss me yet?! I'm emailing you from the study in our dorm. It's a room full of desks where we can do our homework and projects and stuff—we're not meant to use our laptops in our rooms until we're older. Whatever.

Did Mum show you the photo I texted her of my dorm room? It's so annoying you don't have your own phone yet. Don't worry though—you'll get one next year, like I did for my last year of primary school. I guess we're stuck emailing until then!

Have you taken over my room yet? You'd better not. And keep Bob off my bed! Just because I'm not there doesn't mean my bedroom turns into the dog's room.

Guess what? Zoe is in my dorm room! I'm soooo happy! There's this other girl, Grace, and she is so funny. She never stops talking—a bit like you! And then there's Violet. I'm not sure about her yet. She's really quiet and she kind of never smiles. I don't know if she's shy or if she just doesn't like us.

There is one girl who *definitely* doesn't like me. Saskia. I totally stuck my foot in it when she heard me laughing at a painting of her old great-grandma. Oops!

Anyway, I'd better go. We're about to go for dinner. It's just Year 7 here today, but tomorrow all the other years come back to school.

Email me back!

Love, Ella

xx

Opulent. That's another word I use in my writing sometimes. It means luxurious or expensive. And that's the word I thought of when I entered our dining hall. It is a massive, cavernous room with high, pitched ceilings. Chandeliers hung from the ceilings and the floor was beautiful, polished, dark wood. Very chic. There were massive, long tables with wooden benches in long rows. The room looked pretty much empty with only Year 7 in there for dinner that night, but I knew once the rest of the school arrived tomorrow it would be a bustling hive of chatter.

As we entered, we lined up along the left wall where the kitchen and service counter were located. I took a tray and moved along the line. A group of women stood behind the counter with ladles, spooning food onto everyone's plates. I think Nanna Kate would have described them as "matronly." I held out my plate and one of them placed a serving of lasagna onto the white porcelain.

"Thank you," I said cheerily. The server didn't smile, already serving Zoe behind me. I shuffled along and received some salad and garlic bread, then walked over to the cutlery containers to fetch a knife and fork.

"Where should we sit?" Zoe asked. We scanned the room until we saw Grace waving wildly from her seat. She had been ahead of us in the line and had already found a place to sit.

"There's Grace—let's go sit with her," Zoe said, racing ahead of me.

As I approached the table my stomach dropped. On the other side was Saskia, flanked by two girls who looked equally annoyed.

"Oh, not there," I whispered to Zoe through clenched teeth, but she didn't hear me. By the time she saw Saskia, she'd already sat down and it was too awkward to move.

"Well, well, well, if it isn't the art critic," Saskia said coolly as I sat down.

Grace looked confused. "Saskia, have you met Ella and Zoe? They're my roomies! Girls, this is Saskia Bellavance. We met on orientation day last year."

Saskia gave me a fake smile.

"And these two are Saskia's roomies," Grace continued. "Portia and Mercedes."

"Hi," Zoe and I chorused.

"So, how are you finding things at Eden?" I asked, trying to make conversation. "It's all pretty new and weird, isn't it?"

"Well, not for *us*," Saskia said. "Portia, Mercedes and I all have sisters in Year 9, so we've been coming to events at this school for years. And as you've already seen, my family has a long history at this college. I've had my name on the list to come here since the day I was born!"

Portia and Mercedes laughed. "Me too!"

"The minute my mum found out I was a girl, they were filling out the Eden forms!" Mercedes said, flicking her black hair over her shoulder.

"When did you put your names down?" Portia asked.

"Probably when I was a baby," laughed Grace.

"I think sometime during primary school—I don't really know," Zoe said, a little uncertain.

"What about you, Ella? Does your family have an Eden history?" Saskia asked coldly.

"Oh, no, not really. We only decided I was coming pretty late last year," I said, my cheeks reddening. Why was I so embarrassed?

"Last year? How on *earth* did you get into Eden if you only put your name down last year? The waiting list is, like, ten years long!" Saskia said frowning.

"Unless she's on a scholarship," Portia interjected.

I flashed a look at Zoe. I'd said to Zoe earlier that I didn't want people knowing I was on a scholarship. I don't really know why—I just felt like people would expect me to be the best at everything if they knew I had the All-Rounder. And I felt a little weird about coming to the school for free.

"Oh, a *scholarship*," Saskia cooed. "How interesting."

"What's a scholarship?" Mercedes asked.

"It's a free spot at the College they give to girls from poor families," Saskia said.

"It is not!" Zoe said. "It's for the smartest, most talented girls they can find!"

Oh, how I loved my BFF (that's Best Friend Forever).

"Yes, but think about it. Why would they give a scholarship to a girl they knew would come anyway? They *say* it's for talent, but really it's just charity." Saskia looked me straight in the eyes.

I looked away, my cheeks burning. I stabbed my fork at my lasagna, pushing a piece around my plate, but not actually picking it up and eating it. The word *charity* stuck in my mind like a piece of gum on the bottom of my shoe. I tried to shake it off, but it hung there like an accusation.

"Who cares anyway?" Grace said, breaking the silence. "That's boring. I want to know all the goss about this school. So, what are some of the Eden secrets? You girls must know if you have sisters here."

Saskia's eyes lit up and she smiled warmly at Grace.

"Well, there's old Montgomery for a start," she whispered, her eyes darting up to look at Ms. Montgomery. We all leaned in closer to hear.

"What about her?" Zoe asked.

"Well, years and years ago, she was engaged to the Eden Head of Science," Saskia whispered. "They were going to get married, right here in the school grounds, but then on the day of the wedding, he disappeared!"

"Ran for his life, more like it," laughed Portia.

"Nobody knew where he went and he was never heard from again," Saskia added.

"Maybe he got cold feet," suggested Grace.

"Or maybe *she* got cold feet. And maybe she was too embarrassed to end the wedding, so she . . . *dealt* with him," Saskia hissed dramatically.

"You mean, killed him? As if!" I laughed.

"Some people say his ghost still haunts the school, wandering the halls at night, trying to find his lost love," Mercedes said in an eerie voice. "You can hear the clinking of the science beakers he carries around."

"Wooooooooo!" Grace wailed. We all cracked up laughing.

"She does seem kind of sad though," I said, glancing over at Ms. Montgomery. She sat by herself at the head of the table. Her brow was furrowed and her beady eyes darted around the room, looking for someone to reprimand. Suddenly, her eyes locked on us. We all jumped and quickly looked down at our meals. Ms. Montgomery frowned.

As I ate my lasagna, I noticed Violet looking for a seat.

"Hey, Violet! Want to sit here?" I called out as she neared us.

Violet shook her head and continued to the end of the bench, which was empty. As she sat down, she picked up the book resting on her meal tray and began to read as she ate. Her body was turned so that her back was facing the rest of the table. As if she was guarding her dinner tray.

"Girls, attention please," Ms. Montgomery's voice boomed from the front of the dining hall.

Everyone immediately stopped talking and looked up. "When you finish, please take your dishes and cutlery to the wash area over there and load it into the trays for the dishwasher. Then I want you all to go back to your dormitory for quiet reading before bed. It's been a big day and you need to rest before the remainder of the school arrives tomorrow."

I gulped. It would be different with all the older girls joining the dorm. And then with school starting on Monday. I wondered if I was going to fit in at Eden. As a scholarship girl, I felt like I had a lot to live up to.

I lay in my new bed, gazing up at the dark ceiling. I could see the moon peeking through the blinds and I knew it was late. I whispered across to Zoe, but all I heard back was her slow, measured breaths. She was definitely asleep.

I crept out of bed and walked past Grace. Her blankets were in a big, tangled mess and her arms and legs were splayed out all over the bed. Violet was curled into a ball, snoring quietly. I tiptoed over to the bay window and sat down on the window-seat cushions. I gently levered open the blinds, just enough to see out but not enough to wake my roommates. It was a clear, dark night, the sky full of stars. The moon shone round and bright. It was beautiful.

My breath fogged against the window as I held my face close to the glass. It reminded me of those long, summer nights we'd enjoyed just last week. It stayed light for so long that Olivia and I would jump on our trampoline after dinner! I could still smell the barbecue. When it finally did get dark, Mum would let us stay up extra late because it was summer. Dad would light the firepit and we would all push plump marshmallows onto sticks and cook them in the flames. I liked mine lightly toasted, but Olivia always burned hers to a crisp. Max was more interested in using his as bait to catch fireflies.

What were they doing right now? Sleeping? Missing me?

A warm tear trickled down my cheek.

I miss you, Olivia.

I breathed a hot puff of air onto the window, fogging it up again. Then I used my index finger to gently write into the fog "E+O."

Suddenly, I heard a gentle clinking sound. It was very soft, but seemed to be getting louder. It sounded like drinking glasses, rattling in the dishwasher. Or perhaps like a tiny, glass mouse, tiptoeing along a frozen lake. Weird.

Clink.

Clink.

Clink.

I thought back to dinner. Saskia could be funny but also mean. Nanna Kate called girls like that "hot-cold girls." She said it's best to avoid them because you never know if they are going to be nice or mean. I definitely had a hot-cold girl in my primary school. I wonder what she's doing now.

Clink.

Clink.

The noise was getting louder. How annoying.

Grace seemed funny. She was going to be a fun friend to have around. I giggled as I thought about Ms. Montgomery staring at us at dinner.

Clink.

That story about her missing fiancé was pretty hilarious.

Clink.

Ghost—ha! I mean, as if there was a ghost walking around carrying glass beakers . . .

GLASS BEAKERS?

The clinking was even louder now. I leapt off the window seat, ran across the room and jumped into bed, just as the clinking noise stopped outside our door. I yanked the covers over my head. Then I heard the door creak open and saw a tiny sliver of light shine into the room. I squeezed my eyes shut tight.

It's not a ghost. It's not a ghost.

The door creaked shut again, and I let out a breath. It was definitely time to sleep.

Chapter 4

I smoothed my hands over my lap, straightening out the little creases in my school dress. The uniform wasn't exactly what I'd choose to wear—it had no flair about it—but it was a smart-looking dress. It had royal-blue stripes running down the teal fabric and white buttons up the front. The sleeves had a nice little cuff, just below the shoulders, and the top of the dress had a white collar. Since it was summer, we were instructed to wear our panama hats whenever we were outside to avoid sun damage. I don't mind this rule because Nanna Kate says too much sun can "wreak havoc on your complexion." *Complexion* is a posh way of saying skin.

The royal-blue blazer always had to be worn in winter, however in summer it was optional when inside the grounds. Although if we were to leave the grounds for any reason, we had to have the blazer on at all times. It seemed like there were lots of rules at this school, and it was going to take me some time to get to know them all. I'd already been in trouble once with Ms. Montgomery, so I had to be careful not to break any other rules. I really didn't want to start my time at Eden College on the wrong foot.

While the older years were arriving back at the dorms after their summer break, the Year 7 girls were taking a tour of the rest of the school. As I walked around the campus with the other students in my year, I thought about what a paradox this place was. A *paradox* is when two opposite things are put together. The school was a funny mix of grand, old-fashioned buildings, made of stone with ornate sculptures and columns, and completely modern interiors. For example, to get to the science labs you had to walk through a big, stone archway with a lion statue at the entrance, but when you got inside it looked like something out of a science show. The room was filled with sleek, long lab benches, high, wooden stools, rows of microscopes, smart boards and cabinets full of glass beakers, test tubes and Bunsen burners. We hadn't done many science experiments in my primary school, so I was pretty excited to try that out at Eden.

We walked back outside the main building and across to the auditorium. Inside, it looked like a concert hall. There was a big stage with plush, velvet curtains and a lectern in the center. We filed in quietly, slightly awed by the size of the room. Each seat was a flip-down one, like they have at the cinema. Grace sidestepped her way along the row toward the center, and Zoe and I followed. We sat down and waited.

"Pretty fancy, hey?" Grace whispered, smiling brightly.

Ms. Montgomery and Mrs. Sinclair walked onto the stage, along with some other teachers. They sat on the chairs behind the lectern. Mrs. Sinclair stepped up to the microphone.

"Welcome again, Year 7," she said brightly. "I trust you all enjoyed your first night at Eden College?"

There was a murmur of agreement among the girls.

"Excellent. You will have noticed the other girls in Years 8 to 12 have been arriving on campus throughout the morning. I hope you will begin to get to know them—they'll be like your big sisters in the dorms," Mrs. Sinclair said. "I have a few announcements to help orientate you all as you formally begin your time here at Eden. Tomorrow, Monday, you will begin your lessons. We will put you into classes, however these classes are only temporary. In the next few weeks you will undergo some testing and, following that testing, we will reform the classes based on your ability."

There was a collective groan from everyone in the auditorium. We hadn't even started our classes yet and we were already being told about tests!

"Now, now," Mrs. Sinclair laughed. "These tests are nothing to be worried about. We are simply working out which classes you will be in so that you can learn at the appropriate pace. It's not a competition."

This didn't seem to cheer anyone up.

"In more exciting news," Mrs. Sinclair continued, "this afternoon we will be holding our clubs and activities fair in the gymnasium, which is inside the sports and aquatic center. This is run by our Year 9 students. Many of our clubs are divided into Juniors and Seniors, and therefore the Year 9 girls will run the clubs for the Juniors in Years 7 to 9. There will be various stalls with information about all the different clubs you can join at the school. None of these clubs are compulsory, but this is your chance to see what is on offer here and think about what you might like to join."

The sound of excited whispers and muttered chatter broke out.

"I hope there's a musical society," Grace beamed. "I'd love to be in a musical!"

"All right, all right," Mrs. Sinclair said, waving her hands for quiet. "You may now go back to your dorm and enjoy some free time before this afternoon's fair. Dismissed!"

Zoe, Grace and I walked in a row on our way back to the dorm.

"Which club do you want to join, Ella?" Grace asked.

I thought for a minute. "Well, I'd like to be in the orchestra. And the dance troupe. And on the gymnastics team. And maybe debate. And I love drama . . ."

"Whoa, slow down, Miss Overachiever," Zoe laughed. "You're not going to have any spare time at all if you do *everything*!"

"And you'll have no time to study and you'll be in the bottom class for everything," a snide voice said from behind us.

Saskia.

"Oh, Saskia, whatever," Grace laughed.

"Didn't you hear Mrs. Sinclair?" Saskia said, pushing her way in between the three of us. "Testing starts in just a few weeks and that will determine which stream you are in for the rest of the year. Mess up those tests and you'll be stuck in the lower class forever."

"Mrs. Sinclair said it's nothing to stress about," Zoe said, annoyed.

"They always *say* that," Saskia said. "But really these are the tests that set the tone for your entire life at Eden. And while it's not *my* problem, I'd hate to be on a scholarship and fail the first tests here. I mean, they can always take scholarships away, you know."

"They do not," Zoe interjected.

"Do too!" Saskia cried. "It happened in my sister's year. A girl on scholarship wasn't performing and they took the scholarship from her. Then she had to leave."

I gulped. Was that true?

"See you at the clubs fair!" Saskia sang as she skipped off ahead of us.

"Don't worry, Ella. She's just trying to get in your head," Zoe said, linking arms with me.

Zoe was right. Saskia probably was just messing with me. But was it also true?

Later that afternoon we wandered down to the gymnasium, where the clubs fair was set up. Inside, there were tables everywhere, with signs on them.

Some were printed out from the computer and others were hand decorated with gel pens and bubble writing. Year 9 girls stood behind each table, handing out pieces of paper. As soon as we walked in the door, Grace ran off to the musical society table to find out what performances were going to be held throughout the year. Zoe and I wandered from table to table, amazed at all the things on offer.

"Ooh, look, Ella!" Zoe gasped. "Robotics!"

Zoe is super at science and math. We did a bit of coding in primary school, and Zoe was really good at that, too. She gently tugged my arm, but I laughed and pulled back.

"Robotics is your thing, Zo. You go sign up. I'm going to keep looking around."

Zoe smiled and trotted off to the robotics table, where a group of Year 9 girls started chatting excitedly to her. I kept walking from table to table.

Fencing. Equestrian. Beekeeping.

I thought back to the Eden College brochures I'd seen last year. There was so much on offer.

49

Almost too much. I wanted to try everything, but I felt really overwhelmed by the choices.

This was also my chance to work out who I wanted to be at Eden. Nanna Kate says sometimes people need a fresh start. I didn't think I needed a fresh start—I was pretty happy with who I was—but there was a hint of adventure about it all. Who is Ella as an Eden Girl?

As I got to the end of the row of stalls, I saw a tall, blond girl with shining blue eyes standing behind a table. She had three other girls with her. She smiled and gently waved to me, beckoning me to come look at her stall. I wandered over.

The sign on the table looked like a page out of a newspaper. The headline read: *Do you love to write?*

My heartbeat quickened slightly and it felt like a balloon was expanding in my chest. A smile crept onto my face. The girl saw it and grinned.

"Hi! What's your name?" she asked.

"Ella. What's this club?"

"This is the school newspaper. It's online, of course," she said. "We're called *Eden Press*. Interested?"

"I don't know," I said slowly. "I've never been part of a newspaper club before. What would I be doing?"

"We cover all the news at Eden! We report on school events, dorm news, school scandals," she said cheekily, raising one eyebrow. "We also do creative writing, advice columns and puzzles and stuff."

My eyes widened. It sounded interesting.

"My name is Ivy, and I'm the Editor of the paper," the girl said. "We'd love some Year 7 girls to join us this year."

"And," another girl at the stand said, "we are looking for our next Junior Journalist. The Junior Journalist will cover all the major news for Year 7 and be in charge of any other Year 7 writers we have in the club."

"How do you decide who gets to be the Junior Journalist?" I asked.

"We'll get the new Year 7 girls to write some practice pieces for us. Best writer can have the job," Ivy said.

"But we all know who the best writer is anyway," a voice said from behind me. Saskia skipped up to the table and wrote her name down on the list to join *Eden Press*.

I rolled my eyes. Did I *really* want to be in a club with Saskia?

I had turned to walk away when I heard Saskia whisper to the other girls, "She probably can't write anyway."

I felt my cheeks redden. How dare she say that? I *loved* to write. In fact, I'd won the creative writing prize at my school speech night last year—out of the entire school. I'd even won a creative writing competition out of the whole *district*. I wasn't going to back down just because of Saskia! I flung myself around and marched back up to the table. I grabbed the pen and wrote my name on the list.

"I'd love to join," I said, as I stared straight into Saskia's eyes. "And I'd love to try out for the position of Junior Journalist."

"That's great!" Ivy said. "The more the merrier. And don't worry, Saskia won't have any unfair advantages," she laughed cheerily.

As I turned to walk away for the second time, I wondered what she meant. Why would Saskia have an unfair advantage? I hadn't taken a step before I felt Saskia lean in close to me and whisper in my ear.

"By the way," she said, her warm breath tickling. "Ivy is my sister."

Then she laughed and skipped away.

Chapter 5

✕ —

From: <u>Ella</u>

Sent: Friday, 3:45 PM

To: <u>Olivia</u>

Subject: Clubs Fair

Hi Olivia,

I can't believe you got Class Captain! That's awesome.

I bet Mum and Dad were soooo happy.

Well, week one as an Eden Girl is done and dusted! And

I survived. We had the clubs fair earlier this week. You

wouldn't believe how much they have going on.

There are so many clubs you would like—a robotics team, a science club and even an inventors' club! You would love it at Eden College. I hope you can come and join me here one day.

I've joined the school orchestra, the gymnastics team and I'm going to have a go at being a reporter for *Eden Press*. It's an online newspaper where we report on school stuff. But Saskia is joining too—UGH!!!!! That's the girl who got me in trouble on my first day. She's super mean. Remind you of anyone from my primary school class??!!

Zoe and I are loving hanging out with our new roomie, Grace. She's totes funny—you'd love her! Violet is still a bit weird though. Yesterday morning, I saw her sneaking outside before breakfast. Where would she go at 7:00 a.m. on her own? Weird, weird, WEIRD.

I'll video call you this weekend.

Love, Ella

xx

PS. I think there might be a ghost in the dorms! Every night I hear it clinking past my room. Soooo creepy.

"So, who has got some ideas for Issue 1?" Ivy asked.

There were a few murmurs among the girls in the room. There were about ten of us in there, ranging from Year 7 to Year 9. The Year 9 girls were sitting at the head of the table with their laptops open, taking notes. Saskia was sitting as close to them as possible, of course.

It was our first meeting of *Eden Press* and we all wanted Issue 1 to go off with a bang.

"Our website data shows that our readership is declining," Ivy said seriously. "The number of girls actually going to the page and downloading the online paper has decreased over the last few terms. I'm hoping this year can be a much better year for the paper. So, what are your ideas?"

"We need a juicy story," someone ventured. "Maybe we could do an exposé on what they *really* put in our food in the dining hall . . ."

"I think you'll find it's just organic beef, Ashley," Ivy said. "Anyone else?"

"The athletics meet is this term," another girl said.

"We can cover that—you know, interview the winners and record breakers?"

Ivy nodded.

"And what about we run some competitions?" someone else offered. "We'll get more readers if they are, like, involved."

"I can work on some more puzzles and things," another person said.

"This is all good, but we need something *more*," Ivy said, frustrated. "What about our new Year 7 members—do any of you have ideas?"

"What about some fashion advice? I could totally get that happening," Saskia said cheerily.

"Fashion advice isn't that interesting when we all wear the same uniform," Ivy answered. Saskia frowned and wrinkled her nose angrily.

"Ella, what do you think?" Ivy asked.

Everyone in the room turned to look at me and waited. I felt my cheeks flush pink.

"Well," I said slowly. "I think we need to find the things that matter to people. Competitions and reports on the athletics meet are all good stuff, but what is it that people really want to read about?"

"Go on," encouraged Ivy.

"Maybe we should address the issues affecting all of us. Like homesickness. Or pressure to perform. And we could find out what is going on in the dorms that people are worried or excited about. That's what I'd want to read anyway," I trailed off. I held my breath for a second, wondering if everyone was about to burst out laughing at me.

"That's exactly what we need," gushed Ivy.

I let out a sigh.

"Right, I want everyone to keep their ears to the ground. Work out what the big issues are in the dorms and let's report on those things. We'll meet again in a week and discuss what has come up," Ivy said. "Good job, Ella," she smiled.

Everyone stood up and collected their things. I snapped shut my notebook and gathered my pens back into my pencil case. The Year 9 girls slapped their laptops closed and zipped them into their cases.

I heard the warning bell sound in the distance, letting us know that lunchtime was going to end in five minutes. Following the other girls out of the meeting room, I stepped into the sunshine and began to walk up the path, smiling lightly. *Eden Press* was going well. I shielded my eyes from the sun as it beat down onto my head—oh, no! I'd left my panama hat in the meeting room. I was supposed to wear it outside at all times, so I had to go back and get it.

As I quietly walked into the meeting room, I heard an angry voice hissing.

"Being the Editor doesn't mean you have to make me look silly in front of everyone."

It was Saskia.

"Saskia, I wasn't trying to make you look silly," Ivy said, shaking her head.

I stepped back behind the doorway.

"Of course you were. You always want to be the best and you can't handle the fact that now that I'm here at Eden as well, I might just shine a bit brighter than you," Saskia spat.

"Come on, Saskia, that's not true."

"Just because you're in the top classes for everything and are Editor of the paper and a prefect of the Juniors, it doesn't mean you're better than me! Mum and Dad will see just how great I can be when I do all those things myself—and more! You just wait till I'm in the top classes and winning all the awards . . ."

"Saskia, wait," Ivy pleaded as Saskia turned angrily away from her.

I jumped and ducked behind the bookcase in the hallway as Saskia stormed out of the room.

I quietly walked into the meeting room where Ivy was sitting at the table with her head in her hands.

"Err . . . sorry, I just need to get my hat," I mumbled awkwardly.

"It's OK, Ella," she said. "I saw you in the doorway. I'm sorry you had to witness that."

"I get it," I said. "I have a younger sister, too. It can be a bit . . . fraught."

Ivy smiled.

"Fraught means very likely to go wrong," I added.

"I know," Ivy laughed.

"Of course you know," I bumbled, feeling foolish. "You're the Editor of the paper—I'd expect you to know what words mean! I'm sorry."

Ivy laughed again, then sighed. "I don't know why Saskia thinks everything is a competition."

"She probably just really admires you," I said as I picked up my hat. "That's what my Nanna Kate says when my sister Olivia is being all competitive and annoying. She says the reason she wants to beat me more than anyone else is because she actually thinks I'm the best."

Ivy nodded. "I guess. Your Nanna Kate sounds like a smart lady."

I smiled. "See you around!"

As I walked back out of the meeting room, I thought about Saskia and Ivy. Maybe they weren't all that different than me and Olivia. It's hard for the younger sister to feel she has to live up to the older sister. And it's hard for the big sister not to take all the limelight just because she's older. But as Nanna

Kate says, there's nothing more precious than a sister. I hoped Saskia realized that. I sure was realizing it more and more now that mine was so far away.

Chapter 6

I held the photo up close to my face and smiled. It was a selfie of me, Olivia and Max. We were at the zoo with our Nanna Kate and we had taken a photo outside the giraffe enclosure. Olivia was doing bunny ears behind my head and Max was making a silly face. I stuck the photo up next to the one of Mum and Dad on the wall above my bed. I tilted my head to the side then shifted the photo so it was on an angle. Much more artistic.

I picked up the next photo from the little box I'd brought with me to Eden College. This one was of our dog, Bob. His mouth was open in a pant and it looked like he had a great big smile on his face. I'm pretty sure the photo was from a camping trip up the coast, as there were remnants of sand on his shiny, black nose. I stuck the photo of Bob underneath the one of me and my siblings.

I plumped up the pillow on my bed and smoothed out the bedspread. We were allowed to have any bedspread we wanted, which was a nice way to express ourselves a little. Grace's bedspread was rainbow colored. Zoe's was white with purple flowers. Violet's was green with black stripes. Mine had my favorite colors—aqua and purple. And I had a special cushion on my bed with the silhouette of a gymnast doing a handstand with her legs in the splits. Underneath the gymnast were the words "Warning: Gymnast. May flip at any time." Max had given it to me for Christmas.

I stood back and looked at my little corner of the room. It was starting to feel a bit more like home. I hadn't had a chance during the first week to decorate my area, but now that it was Friday afternoon, I finally had some downtime.

I looked at the photos of my family and sighed. I felt a small lump rise in my throat, but I swallowed it down.

"It's gone. I've looked everywhere and it's gone!" Zoe said, exasperated.

"What's gone?" Grace asked, looking up from the book she was reading.

"My necklace. My precious necklace!"

"Check your drawers," I said.

"I did. And it's GONE!" Zoe burst into tears. I moved over and gave her a hug.

"Don't cry, Zoe," Grace said softly.

"We'll find it," I said, patting her back soothingly.

"That necklace was from my nonna. She gave it to me so I would have a reminder of her at Eden. I have to find it," Zoe sobbed.

"Are you OK, Zoe?" a small voice asked from the doorway. It was Violet.

"She's lost her precious necklace," Grace said.

"I didn't lose it," Zoe snapped. "I think it was stolen."

"Oh, that's terrible," Violet said. Her cheeks flushed

pink. She looked around the room awkwardly. "I'm sure you just misplaced it."

"I didn't!" Zoe sniffed. "I kept it here, on my dresser, in this special little box."

An alarm beeped on Violet's watch. "Oh, I have to go," she said hurriedly, and she rushed out of the room.

Weird.

"We should tell Ms. Montgomery," I said, giving Zoe another hug.

"I don't want to go to her," Zoe sniffled. "She'll say I've been careless and lost it."

I thought for a minute. If the necklace *was* stolen, we probably should report it. I looked out of our dorm room and into the hallway. Ivy was just walking past.

"Ivy!" I called and beckoned her to come into our room.

"Ivy, this is Zoe," I said. "Zoe, Ivy is a Juniors' Prefect. She'll know what to do."

"What's up?" Ivy asked gently, sitting down on the window seat.

Zoe explained about her necklace, fresh tears

springing from her eyes. She told Ivy how close she is to her nonna and how the necklace was her special piece of home. Ivy nodded sympathetically.

"And you're sure you haven't lost it?" Ivy asked.

"I'm sure," Zoe said firmly.

"OK, I'm going to write all this down and log it. I'll also bring this up at our Prefect meeting in a couple of days. In the meantime, I want you to have a really good look for the necklace, Zoe. If it doesn't turn up in a couple of days, I'll go with you to speak to Ms. Montgomery about it. We need to be careful we don't jump to conclusions about it being stolen. That will send everyone into a panic. So can you just keep looking for a day or two? Does that sound like a plan?"

Zoe nodded sadly.

I looked up and saw Saskia in our doorway, a confused and annoyed look on her face. She continued up the hallway with a huff.

Ivy rolled her eyes and stood up. "Let me know how you do." She walked out of the room with a wave.

I looked at my best friend's sad face. Her dark-brown

eyes were red and puffy. I put my hand on her leg. This was the first time since moving to Eden College that I'd seen Zoe upset. Even on those first couple of nights when heaps of girls were teary and homesick, Zoe wasn't. Zoe just copes. She can handle pressure and turn it into something positive. When I get a bit dramatic (which only happens SOMETIMES), she is always the one to talk me back down to reality and see sense, whatever the situation. It was unusual for me to be the comforter when it came to the two of us. And I hated seeing her so down.

I looked up at Grace and shrugged, silently asking her what we could possibly do to help.

"You know, I think we need a bit of fun to cheer you up, Zoe. It's the weekend, and just because we live at school, it doesn't mean we can't loosen up a bit," Grace said, jumping off the bed.

"What do you suggest?" I asked Grace, as Zoe wiped her eyes.

"It's Friday night! We need to live a bit. Let's sneak down to the common room for a midnight feast!" Grace laughed.

"What would we feast on—bread and milk from the kitchen?" Zoe said sarcastically.

"No . . . THIS!" Grace opened her bottom drawer with a flourish and revealed a stash of candy and chocolate.

"Where did that come from?" I laughed.

"My dad just got back from a business trip to the US and brought home all this American candy. So I brought it here. For emergencies." Grace smiled impishly.

"Won't we get in trouble, sneaking downstairs at night? Why not just have it here in the dorm room?" Zoe asked.

"That's boring. Plus we want the other girls to come too, don't we? Year 7 bonding time?" Grace asked.

I looked at her, unsure. I didn't want to get into trouble. But then I looked at Zoe, who was smiling despite her red, watery eyes.

"Let's do it," I said, making up my mind.

"I'll spread the word," Grace said, jiggling up and down with excitement. "Tonight. Midnight. The common room."

"Ella!" a voice hissed. "Get up! ELLA!"

It was Grace, standing over me with a flashlight. I rubbed my sleepy eyes and rolled over in bed. The clock on the desk flashed 11:52 p.m.

"I don't want to anymore, Grace. Go back to bed," I moaned as I snuggled deeper under my covers.

Grace pulled back my blanket in one swift movement.

"Get UP!" she hissed.

I rolled my sleepy body over and hung my legs over the edge of the bed. Grace had already brought over my slippers and robe, which were sitting on the floor, ready for our escapade.

I could see a sliver of light glowing through the blinds.

On the other side of the room, Zoe was sleepily pulling her robe across her body. Violet snored on. She had said earlier that afternoon that candy wasn't "her thing" and that she didn't want to come to the

Common Room Midnight Feast (or CRMF, as we had code-named it).

Grace grabbed her flashlight, then slowly opened the door. She looked up and down the hallway, switched on the flashlight, then beckoned for us to follow her. I heard the quiet padding of footsteps as girls from the other rooms giggled their way up the hall. We all tiptoed downstairs and let ourselves into the common room.

It was dark and cold in the stark moonlight—the beanbags were stiff and chilly. We plonked ourselves in a circle.

There were about fifteen of us who had decided to join the CRMF. Everyone else had said it was too dangerous and that we were silly to try it. Surprisingly, Saskia, Portia and Mercedes were there. I thought Saskia would have been way too much of a goody-goody to sneak out at night. But Saskia constantly surprised me.

"I hereby declare the first Year 7 CRMF open!" Grace giggled, as she pretended to cut an invisible ribbon in the air.

We all laughed but then shushed each other, aware

that Ms. Montgomery's room was only down the hall.

Grace pulled out the candy from under her robe and dumped it in the middle of the circle. We all swooped on it like seagulls.

"So, what now?" Zoe asked in a whisper. "Ghost stories?"

"Truth or Dare, I say," Saskia said.

"Yeah, Truth or Dare!" Portia and Mercedes chorused.

"OK, I'm first!" Saskia declared in her pompous way. *Pompous* means self-important.

"Let's flick this chocolate bar in the air," Grace said. "If it lands faceup, it's Truth. But if it lands facedown, it's Dare."

We all agreed.

Grace flipped the chocolate bar up into the air and it landed on the carpet, faceup.

"TRUTH!" we all screamed.

"SSSSSHHHH!" Grace hissed. "OK, who has a truth question for Saskia?"

"What's your biggest fear?" Zoe asked.

Saskia thought. "Spiders," she said.

"Really?" Zoe asked. "That's your true biggest fear?"

"Yep."

"Are you sure it isn't your beautiful hair turning green?" Portia teased.

"Or your clothes being mismatched?" Mercedes laughed.

Saskia jokingly punched Mercedes in the arm.

"Or not being in the top class for everything?" I laughed, joining in.

Saskia looked at me and her smile vanished. She took a sharp breath and tucked her hair behind her ears. Then she frowned, shook her head and quickly grabbed the chocolate bar, flicking it into the air.

"This is for you, Ella," she said. She sounded annoyed. Had I said something wrong?

The chocolate spun through the air then landed facedown. Dare.

"I dare you," Saskia jumped in before anyone else could speak, "to sneak up the hallway, touch Ms. Montgomery's doorknob, then sneak back."

"No way!" I protested. "She'll hear me! The floorboards creak!"

"That's your dare!" Saskia said.

I looked around at all the faces staring back at me in the darkness.

"OK," I agreed finally, standing up.

I walked out through the big double doors of the common room and began to tiptoe slowly up the hallway. I tried to walk nice and close to the wall, as the floorboards seemed to squeak less there. I turned around about halfway to see multiple giggling faces watching me from the common room doorway.

SQUEAK!

I paused, wincing, but nothing happened so I continued on.

The hallway became darker as I approached Ms. Montgomery's room, which was toward the back of the house.

The grandfather clock was so loud in the quiet hallway.

Tick.

Tock.

Tick.

Tock.

SQUEAK!

Ugh, another floorboard. I froze. I was within a couple of feet of Ms. Montgomery's room. Was that a shuffling noise inside? I stood as still as a statue. No, it must not have been.

I took a couple more steps and reached out my hand, ready to touch the doorknob.

Suddenly, the door flung open!

Ms. Montgomery was standing tall in her bathrobe, looking down at me with my outstretched hand. Her face looked ice-cold and her brow was furrowed angrily.

"Ella!" she gasped. "What are you doing?"

My mind raced. How was I going to get out of this one?

I heard the girls in the common room shuffle back from the doorway. Ms. Montgomery's head shot up, craning her neck to see what the noise was that she had heard up ahead. If Ms. Montgomery went to the common room, we were dead meat.

I slowly walked past Ms. Montgomery so she had to turn away from the common room to keep facing me.

"Mum, is it breakfast?" I mumbled sleepily.

Ms. Montgomery looked confused.

Behind her, I saw the girls file one by one out of the common room and back up the stairs to the dorm rooms. If I could just keep her looking the other way for a couple more seconds, she wouldn't see them.

"Can I have pancakes?" I asked in a slow, sleepy voice.

"Ella, are you . . . are you sleepwalking?" Ms. Montgomery said, frowning.

"Is it time for ballet, Mum?" I mumbled in my best dream voice.

Ms. Montgomery shook her head and took me by the arm. "Ella, come back to bed. It's not morning and you are sleepwalking."

"Can I go swimming today?" I murmured as I let Ms. Montgomery lead me up the stairs. She walked me into my room, where Zoe and Grace were already tucked back up in their beds.

She gently helped me onto my bed and pulled the covers over me.

"Go to sleep," she whispered, as she tucked me in tightly.

Ms. Montgomery took a quick look around the room. Satisfied everyone was fast asleep, she turned and left, quietly shutting the door behind her.

I let out a huge sigh of relief.

Grace and Zoe burst out laughing, muffling the sound with their pillows.

"Thanks for saving us!" Grace giggled.

I rolled my eyes and shook my head. That was enough excitement for one night.

Chapter 7

× —

From: <u>Ella</u>

Sent: Wednesday, 5:40 PM

To: <u>Olivia</u>

Subject: Scandal!

Hi Olivia!

Thanks for sending me the new *Millie Mysteries* book! I can't wait to read it. I'll let you know if it's as good as the first ones. How's everything at home?

Things here at Eden are going great. Sometimes I feel like I've lived here for years! All the girls are getting along really well. Oh, except for the latest scandal.

Zoe couldn't find her precious necklace from her nonna. She said she didn't lose it, so we told Ivy, a Juniors' Prefect, that we thought it was stolen. Since then, other things have been going missing from the Year 7 dorm. A girl called Annabelle has had her watch stolen. And another girl named Chloe says her silk scarf has gone missing. She got it from her aunt who lives in Paris, so it was totally chic and special.

Everyone is starting to blame each other. I've made sure all my precious things are locked in my drawer. I've heard a rumor that they are going to have to lock all our bedrooms in the daytime. We've got a meeting about it with our housemistress and the headmistress later.

Email me soon!

Love, Ella

xx

All of Year 7 was sitting together in the common room after classes—some on the floor, some on the couches and some on beanbags. There was an ominous mood in the room—that means the feeling that something bad was coming. A bit like gray clouds before a storm or when the phone rings in the middle of the night with news about your great-grandma.

I was gazing at the paintings on the common room wall. There was one of a field peppered with white rabbits, which always made me think of my Nanna Kate.

Nanna Kate once told me about the summer she spent in an Italian circus. She used to be a good gymnast, just like me, so she was really strong and bendy. When she was at university, she traveled to Italy with her best friend over a summer break. They needed to make some money and met some people who were in a traveling circus in Tuscany. When they found out my Nanna Kate could do cool gymnastics tricks, they asked if she'd like to be part of the show while it was in town. She did tumbling with the acrobats and learned to juggle.

Nanna Kate said there was a magician named Emerald who could do amazing tricks. She did this one trick where she put a big, slithering snake into a bag. When she opened the bag at the end of the trick, out came five bunnies, as white as the purest snow. Nanna Kate never found out how the trick was done, but every night there was a snake at the beginning of the show and bunnies at the end. When Nanna Kate asked Emerald about it, she just told her that things aren't always what they seem to be.

I looked around the room at the girls in my year. It was so funny to think that I would be spending the next six years with these people—that we'd go from being twelve-year-olds to almost-adults together. It's like they were my sisters. Tight friendships were already forming—some girls were resting on beanbags together and there was a long train of girls sitting in a conga line, braiding each other's hair. Zoe and Grace were squished on a couch with me. I saw Violet sitting over by the wall with her earbuds in. Everything looked normal, but something was up.

"Attention, everyone," Ms. Montgomery said as she glided into the room. Behind her came Mrs. Sinclair, who was looking unusually grave. They shut the big double doors behind them.

"We are holding this meeting with you in the common room because this is where we relax, like any normal family," Mrs. Sinclair said. "And that is what we are—a family. So you can imagine my sadness to hear that there have been thefts among our Year 7 students."

The girls began to murmur between themselves.

"This is very serious. We have reason to believe this is only a Year 7 problem, as all the missing items are from the Year 7 floor. We imagine it would be easier for someone living on that floor to be taking items from that floor," Ms. Montgomery continued on from Mrs. Sinclair.

"We want to give the culprit the opportunity to come clean," Mrs. Sinclair said. "If you come to my office with the items, I would love to talk to you about why it is you've taken them. But I will also be gracious—it's a big deal moving away from home to boarding school. I understand this can have an effect on you. And I'm here to help." She smiled her characteristic warm smile.

"Now, go and get yourselves ready for dinner. I'm hoping the culprit will have come clean within the next 24 hours. Otherwise we are going to have to put in place some very inconvenient precautions, which none of you will enjoy," Mrs. Sinclair said.

Everybody stood up with glum faces. It was horrible to think there could be a thief in our midst. And this was affecting everybody.

I suddenly had a thought.

"Mrs. Sinclair," I said, walking up to the headmistress. "Can I talk to you for a moment?"

"Yes, of course. Let's sit over on the couch, Ella," she said. I loved how Mrs. Sinclair knew every girl in the school by name.

As the other girls filed out of the common room, I sat with Mrs. Sinclair. It felt like sitting with Nanna Kate.

"How are you settling in, Ella?" she asked warmly.

"Oh, I love it here, I really do!" I said. "There's so much to do and be involved in. Which brings me to my question."

"Go on," she said.

"I've joined *Eden Press* and we've been talking about writing stories about things that really matter to the girls. Readership is dropping and I think this is possibly due to us not being . . . not being relevant enough," I said, trying to sound as professional as I could.

Mrs. Sinclair's mouth turned up into a small smile.

"So, I was wondering if I could write about the thefts," I said.

"Oh, Ella, I'm not sure about that," she said, frowning. "We certainly don't want accusations being thrown around. And we don't want panic either. Do you think this is really a good idea?"

"Well, I think this is what matters to us—we all want to feel like we are safe here and nobody likes to think their stuff is in danger of being stolen. It's important, don't you think?"

Mrs. Sinclair tipped her head to one side slightly, thinking.

"And," I continued, "what if I interviewed the people with items missing and gave the story a personal feel. The thief might even read it and be convinced to turn herself in!"

Mrs. Sinclair sat silent for a few seconds. Then she slapped both her hands on her thighs. "OK, yes, Ella!"

I smiled a big smile.

"But," she cautioned, "this is on the condition that you do not accuse anybody of the crimes. Innocent until proven guilty, yes? No trial by media."

I nodded enthusiastically. "Definitely not," I assured her. "This will be a personal piece giving a voice to the victims."

Mrs. Sinclair nodded and patted me on the shoulder. She stood up and headed out the double doors.

YES!

This was my chance to write a really exciting and relevant piece for *Eden Press*. It was going to get me the role of Junior Journalist for sure.

I bounded out of the common room, up the stairs and burst into my dorm room. Rifling through my drawers, I found my special notebook and pen. I needed to start investigating.

Right now.

Chapter 8

Zoe's eyes were shining. And I knew exactly why—we were having our first science lesson in a real laboratory. Now that we were halfway through our second week and all settled in, it was time to hit the labs. In primary school, we did plenty of science. But it was just in our normal classroom with our regular teacher. Our experiments never really went beyond using magnets or mixing colors. Pretty tame. But I knew here at Eden we would be using actual scientific equipment, like Bunsen burners and test tubes and chemicals.

I wasn't that excited because science isn't my thing.

That is NOT because I am a girl. Oh no, it's not. Nanna Kate says she hates how people think writing is for girls and science is for boys. I know that's wrong, wrong, WRONG because my Nanna Kate has a PhD. That means she's a doctor. Not a doctor like the one you go to for medicine—it means she has a doctorate in a special subject. And my Nanna Kate? She is a doctor of science. When she was at university, she studied microbiology. I think that has something to do with tiny germs and stuff, and it was super important. She did all this research into human cells and disease, and she was even part of a team that created a new vaccination.

So girls DO do science.

Just not so much me.

Zoe is a science whiz. She's so good at math and science that she even won the Year 6 prize for it. And Olivia is really keen on experiments and inventions and that kind of thing. It's her passion. Kind of like writing is my passion. Nanna Kate says your passion is the thing that makes your heart sing. My heart sings when I find the right words to properly convey all my feelings and emotions. Olivia's heart sings when she finds out why toilet paper has a scent but tissues don't. She likes answers. I like poetry. Each to their own, I guess.

We all sat behind long, white lab benches on high stools. I sat between Zoe and Grace and behind Saskia, Portia and Mercedes. Up at the front was another long, white bench for the teacher. Behind it was an amazing-looking smart board, which was lit up and ready to go.

The bell had rung for morning classes ten minutes ago and we'd all shuffled into the science lab for our first class. But there was no sign of the teacher. We all whispered to each other in confusion because Eden teachers were *never* late.

Suddenly, the door swung open with a bang and a figure bustled into the room in a mad flurry. It was a short man with frizzy hair, which blew about in a frenzy around his face. He wore round glasses and had a long, unbuttoned, white lab coat, which flapped about his thin body. He had a bright, polka-dot tie, which didn't really match his striped shirt. He was muttering under his breath, "I'm late, I'm late, I'm late," just like the white rabbit from *Alice in Wonderland*.

"Right," he said, as he patted his chest pockets, clearly looking for something. He stopped and thought for a second and then, as he suddenly remembered, pulled a remote out of his back pocket for the smart board.

"I am . . ." He stopped as if he'd momentarily forgotten his own name. "I am Professor Wendell," he said at last. "And I am your science teacher!"

We all sat in silence. He stared at us, as though unsure what to do next.

"Right, right, right," he said, as he bundled through some papers on the desk. "Today, we are going to start with an experiment!"

Zoe squealed quietly.

"This term we are studying chemical reactions," he continued.

Zoe squealed again.

"And we are going to start with an exothermic reaction. Anyone know what that is?" Professor Wendell asked.

Zoe's hand flew up into the air. Professor Wendell

pointed to her.

"A reaction that creates light or heat," Zoe said with a big smile on her face.

"Well done," Professor Wendell smiled. "And today, we will create our own exothermic reaction. This chemical reaction will also show us what a catalyst is. Anyone know that already?"

Zoe's hand shot up again.

"Anyone *else* know?" Professor Wendell asked.

Nobody moved.

"Yes, you again then," he said, pointing to Zoe.

"It's a substance that helps along a chemical reaction," Zoe said.

"Indeed," Professor Wendell nodded. "For this experiment, we will use yeast as a catalyst. Once we mix it together with our other ingredients, we will get a very foamy result," he smiled. "Now, when you come and collect the chemical component, make sure you take this one," he said, pointing to a white bottle, "and not this one," pointing to a red bottle. "The red bottle is a higher concentration that we will use later for a bigger result, but that needs to be done by an adult . . . outside!"

Professor Wendell told us to form groups of three and then explained the equipment we would need. We had to wear gloves and protective eye goggles, which made the experiment seem way more exciting and dangerous. We were instructed to collect a small amount of a special chemical to take back to our desks and put into a glass flask with some dishwashing liquid. We were then to mix the yeast in some water, which we were going to add to our chemical. We also added a food coloring of our choice, which was going to make the special foam a pretty color. Grace, Zoe and I formed a group and collected our equipment.

"It's important you follow the instructions very carefully," Professor Wendell said, as we all set up our experiments at our benches.

It was Grace's job to measure out the chemical, while Zoe and I mixed the yeast.

"Have you guys studied for the streaming tests?" Grace asked.

"A bit," I said. "I should probably do more, but I've been thinking a lot about my *Eden Press* article." I suddenly felt a bit nervous. Maybe I *was* focusing on *Eden Press* too much. What if I didn't do well in the streaming tests? Would I lose my scholarship like Saskia said?

I spooned the yeast into the water and began to mix it around.

"Grace, are you reading the instructions?" Zoe asked as she eyed Grace pouring the chemical into the flask.

Grace waved her hand dismissively as she continued to talk. And talk. And talk. Grace is one of those girls that could talk underwater, as Nanna Kate would say.

In front of us, Saskia, Portia and Mercedes let out a delighted squeal as they added the yeast to their experiment. Immediately, thick coils of foam came bubbling out of their flask and into the sink, which was embedded in the bench.

Professor Wendell clapped excitedly. "Isn't it great?" he laughed.

Another group farther down our bench had the same

reaction as their blue-colored foam rose out of the flask and spilled over into their sink.

"OK, our turn!" Zoe said, picking up the yeast mixture. "You definitely collected the right chemical, didn't you, Grace?"

"Yeah, yeah. Three, two, one, go!" Grace laughed as she grabbed the yeast mixture from Zoe and dumped it into the flask.

BANG!

Our flask exploded and shot a massive tube of foam upward, like an erupting volcano. It came out with such force, Zoe, Grace and I screamed and ducked under the bench. The bright-pink foam kept shooting upward, coating the classroom ceiling in pink bubbles. Saskia, Portia and Mercedes screamed in horror.

"Everyone, outside!" Professor Wendell yelled, as girls started screaming and running around the lab in a wild panic.

The foam continued rolling off the bench in coils.

"Don't touch it!" Professor Wendell yelled. "You used the wrong chemical! It's very dangerous!"

Once he'd said the word "dangerous," the whole class screamed even louder and we joined them as they ran out the door in a thunderous stampede.

Once our experiment had stopped foaming, we cautiously poked our heads back into the lab. Our foam was everywhere—and there was a big, pink stain on the ceiling.

"Oops," Grace whispered.

Chapter 9

I sat on the lawn at lunchtime, gazing at my chicken wrap. It was nice and all, but it was nothing like the lunches Mum would make me in primary school. I remember when I was really little, she used to cut the crusts off my sandwiches, then cut them into the shape of stars or hearts with a cookie cutter. I turned the wrap over in my hands. I really missed my mum.

"Ella, please report to Mrs. Sinclair's office, thank you," the loudspeaker crackled.

I jolted to attention as my name was called. I looked at Zoe and Grace with wide eyes—was I in trouble?

"Want us to come?" Grace offered.

"No, I think it's OK," I mumbled. But inside I was nervous. I wondered what Mrs. Sinclair wanted to see me about. It couldn't be about the science lab mishap earlier that day, otherwise she would have called Grace and Zoe up too.

I walked from where we were eating on Centenary Lawn, up the path and around past the sports and aquatic center, toward the administration building.

The hot sun beat down, seeping through my thin, summer dress. I had my panama hat on but could still feel the intense warmth sink through into my scalp. I pulled my ponytail around my shoulder, rifling my fingers through the hot, sweaty strands of hair that stuck to my neck.

I passed the fountain in the central courtyard and wished I could throw off my dress and jump in with wild abandon, just in my underpants. That's what Olivia would do. But that's definitely not something an Eden Girl would do, for sure. It made me think back to the time Dad got a long piece of tarp and stretched it out, down our backyard. I was only little when we bought the house, but I remember the real estate agent saying in a sympathetic voice, "It is a sloping block, I'm afraid," like that was a really bad thing. But Dad said that made it the perfect backyard for sliding and he reckons that was the tipping point for buying the house. I'm not sure that's totally true, but he was right about it being the perfect yard for a homemade waterslide.

Every summer we would stretch out the tarp and lather it up with dishwashing soap. Then we'd use the sprinkler to create the most epic backyard waterslide. Dad would always run and launch himself down it on his stomach—he'd look just like a penguin shooting across the ice on its tummy. It was so funny.

I smiled.

As I approached the administration block, my smile faded and little butterflies began to dance around in my stomach. I walked up the steps slowly and let myself in through the glass door. The lady at reception smiled over the desk.

"May I help you?" she asked.

"I was paged to see Mrs. Sinclair," I said in a shaky voice.

The receptionist bit her lip slightly, in what appeared to be a stifled giggle. I didn't think it was funny.

She walked through to the back office while I waited.

"Come through," she said, ushering me behind the desk and into Mrs. Sinclair's office.

I'd only been in her office once before—when I came to Eden College for my interview last year. I couldn't imagine why I had been called back now.

The office was large, and behind Mrs. Sinclair's desk was a huge window. It looked out onto the plush, green field where some girls were practicing hockey. On either side of the window were bookshelves, lined with many different types of books. Her desk was large, made of dark wood, and looked heavy and expensive.

Mrs. Sinclair sat behind her desk. She looked over her glasses at me. "Please sit," she urged.

I took a seat on one of the leather chairs opposite her.

"Don't worry, you're not in trouble," she chuckled.

I immediately felt my shoulders relax a little.

On Mrs. Sinclair's desk were several photographs of her at varying ages. In some she looked young—her now short, silver hair nowhere to be seen and long, golden hair in its place. In each photo she was hugging a different dog, sometimes two. They varied in size and breed—one was a golden retriever like my dog, Bob, another was small and white. Mrs. Sinclair followed my eyes.

"My dogs," she said, smiling. "I've had many over the years. I never had children of my own, so my dogs always hold a special place in my heart."

I nodded.

"But I've come to realize that I do have children of my own in a way. My students. Each one is special to me," she said. She shook her head lightly and became businesslike. "Now, Ella, are you still reporting on the thefts in the Year 7 dormitory?" she asked.

I nodded. "Yes, I've interviewed Zoe and Annabelle. But I'm also trying to make sure I get all the facts just right."

Mrs. Sinclair nodded. "I've been thinking about what you said—about giving the culprit an insight into the effect of what they have done. And I think you are right."

"OK," I said uncertainly.

"The thievery has moved beyond the dorms," Mrs. Sinclair said.

"Oh, no!" I replied.

"Yes. Last night, my office was broken into. We know because the window was open when we came in this morning, and I always close up before I leave."

"What did they take?" I asked.

"Look here—this is my shelf of Eden's most prized trophies."

I looked and saw a row of beautiful trophies in varying sizes. They all had names and dates engraved on them and they all looked very important.

"There is one small but very precious trophy missing from this collection," Mrs. Sinclair said, gesturing to an empty spot on the shelf. "It's the House trophy, for the winning House at the end of the year. It's not a huge trophy, which is perhaps why the thief chose to steal it. It could be easily concealed under a jacket or in a backpack. But it's a trophy that's special to the school, donated by one of our headmistresses who has since passed away."

"Oh."

"I would like you to interview me about the trophy, Ella. I'd like you to write about why this trophy is special and include an appeal to the criminal to bring it back."

"I can do that," I said eagerly. This was exactly the kind of scoop I needed for my piece.

"Can you come back tomorrow, at lunchtime, to see me? Bring your notebook?" Mrs. Sinclair asked.

I nodded excitedly.

"All right, then. The bell has gone so take this late note to class with you so you don't get into trouble." She winked as she scribbled on a piece of paper.

I stood up, left Mrs. Sinclair's office and went out into the sunshine. I put on my panama hat and walked across the courtyard toward the classrooms. The outside area was pretty quiet, with everyone in class. I only passed a couple of girls here and there, on their way to the office or maybe the auditorium. As I dawdled up the path (let's face it—I wasn't in a *huge* rush to get to class since it was such a nice day), I saw Violet come out of the main building entrance.

"Hi, Violet," I said, stopping in front of her.

"Oh, hi, Ella," she said nervously. "What are you doing out of class?"

"I was just talking to Mrs. Sinclair. I'm reporting on the thefts for the school paper."

Violet's cheeks were flushed pink and her eyes darted about.

"Where are you going?" I asked.

"Nowhere . . . I mean, obviously somewhere . . . but nowhere special. I mean, I just had to run an errand for Ms. Montgomery. Just quickly," she mumbled.

"Do you need me to come with you? I'm in no hurry to get back to class," I giggled.

Violet's eyes widened. "Thanks, Ella, but no need. I'm fine. In fact, I'd better go right now," she said quickly, as she hurried off.

"Hey, Violet?" I called after her.

Violet stopped in her tracks and turned around slowly. "Come sit with us at dinner tonight, OK?"

Violet's eyes met mine. She stared intently at me for a couple of seconds before looking away.

"That'd be nice," she whispered, before turning and running up the path.

She sure is a funny one, I thought to myself. We'd been at Eden College for a couple of weeks now and she'd barely said three sentences to me. Every time we tried to talk to her, she always made some excuse to get away from the conversation. It was like she didn't want to be our friend, yet there was something sad and lonely in her eyes that seemed to want us to reach out. I didn't quite understand.

She seemed so fragile.

As I walked along, I saw a small bird's nest sitting on the branch of a tree. It reminded me of a little bird that Olivia, Max and I found in our backyard. It was just a baby. It had been rejected by its mother but wasn't quite big enough to fend for itself. We made it a special home in a cardboard box, with a cozy blanket. And we researched what food types were appropriate for a hatchling. But when we went back to get it from under the tree, it was gone. It was too small to fly and couldn't have made it far if it had tried to walk away. Dad had said that it had probably been taken by the neighbor's cat. Olivia cried and said we shouldn't have left it on its own. But I told her maybe its mother took it back—it might be at home and happier than it would have been with us anyway. That cheered Olivia up a lot and she drew a beautiful picture of our bird flying high in the sky with its family.

I'd really believed that the bird's mother had come back for it. I hadn't thought about it for ages. But now, as I walked along the path of my high school, it struck me: maybe Dad had been right.

Chapter 10

The next day, I took my notebook and pen and headed to Mrs. Sinclair's office at lunchtime. I'd thought about bringing my favorite pen with the purple fluff ball on the end, but I figured that wasn't very professional. So I selected a sensible, black pen, which I could click in and out as I pondered big thoughts. That's what always happened in the *Millie Mysteries* books that I liked to read. Whenever she was thinking deep, ponderous thoughts she would *click*, *clickety*, *click* her pen until she had an epiphany. That's a moment of realization when you suddenly know the answers to your deepest questions. Like a big *ping* in your mind.

I smiled at the receptionist, who waved me through, then quietly walked up to Mrs. Sinclair's door and knocked three firm but polite knocks.

"Come in," Mrs. Sinclair's voice said from inside.

"Hello, Ella," she greeted me, with a smile. "Would you like some tea? I've just made a pot. It's decaf," she winked.

"Oh, yes, that would be lovely, thank you," I said, taking a seat in front of her desk.

Mrs. Sinclair pulled out two little china teacups from the cabinet behind her desk and poured the steaming hot tea into the cups. She added milk and offered me sugar, of which I took one cube.

"This reminds me of having tea with my Nanna Kate," I said to her. "Nanna Kate says that tea is a 'balm for the soul.' I'm not sure exactly what that means, but she reckons that if all the world leaders sat around together with a pot of tea, many of the world's problems would be sorted out by the end of the day."

"Your Nanna Kate sounds like someone I would get

along with," Mrs. Sinclair chuckled.

I nodded, then put on my VSC (that's Very Serious Conversation) face.

"So, can you tell me a bit more about this trophy that went missing?" I asked Mrs. Sinclair, with my pen poised over my open notebook.

"Well, Ella," she said, gazing out the window, "we all know that the world is full of . . . of stuff, really. Items that crowd our lives—things we think we need which we really don't. But there are also things that have immense sentimental value—they are more than just *stuff*."

I scribbled frenziedly. *Sentimental value*.

"And the House trophy was a special thing of sentimental value to the Eden community. You see, the previous headmistress before me—the one who donated the trophy—was someone very close to me," Mrs. Sinclair said.

"Can I ask who?"

"Yes, she was my aunt. She was the one who got me a job at Eden College as a teacher. I was young and keen and excited about teaching the girls here. And she was such a passionate person. Passionate about education. Passionate about literature. Passionate about changing lives."

I nodded as I continued to scribble.

"She taught well into her old age, always inspiring the girls, faculty, and staff to be the best they could be. Do you know what our school motto is, Ella?" Mrs. Sinclair asked.

I thought back to the school emblem. Underneath it were words in a language I didn't know.

"It's in Italian, isn't it?" I asked.

"No, my dear, Latin. Some people think Latin is a dead language, just because it isn't spoken anymore. But Latin is like a key—it is a language which opened the doors to our own language, with all its richness. Our school motto is, *In Meliora Contende*. Can you say it?"

"*In Mel . . .*" I began.

"*Meliora Contende*," Mrs. Sinclair finished.

I let the words roll around my tongue. *In Meliora Contende*. "What does it mean?" I asked.

"It means, *Strive for Better Things*. But it also means that the good you do will yield more good things."

I nodded, thinking about the meaning.

"And that is what my aunt taught the girls. She taught them to always try their best and to always seek to do good in a world that isn't always right," Mrs. Sinclair said, taking a sip of her tea. "And so, when she passed away, we made a new House trophy. It was called the Meliora Trophy, and is very precious to me and to the school."

I continued to scribble down notes.

"So, how do you *feel* about it being stolen?" I asked. Ivy had said that good journalists always get to the emotion of a piece.

"Well, I feel very sad, Ella. Because theft is the very opposite to everything my aunt, and indeed our whole school motto, stands for."

"The antithesis, you might say?" I probed. That's a fancy word for opposite.

Mrs. Sinclair let out a chuckle and nodded. "You are a smart cookie, aren't you, Ella?" But then she stopped speaking and stared out the window, into the distance.

I paused in my scribbling and looked at Mrs. Sinclair. She really did look sad. This wasn't just another trophy to her. This was something that represented her aunt. And the school she loved.

"Do you have any more information on your aunt—maybe some other things I can read about her? Maybe I could do a profile on her?" I asked.

"Oh, that would be so lovely, Ella. I actually have some newspaper clippings about her. But alas, they are in my filing cabinet over there," Mrs. Sinclair said, nodding toward the wooden filing drawers in the corner of her office. "Frustratingly, I lost my key just this week! So silly of me—I always keep it in my top drawer here, but I must have taken it out."

Still in reporter mode, I wrote that down in my notes.

"But don't worry—I'll ask the handyman to come and open the lock for me, and when he does I will show the newspaper articles to you," she assured me.

I took my last sip of tea and thanked Mrs. Sinclair. Having tea with her felt like a little piece of home.

"I look forward to reading your piece," Mrs. Sinclair said, as I gathered my notes together.

"Thank you for your time," I said, standing up.

As I walked out the door, I thought about Mrs. Sinclair's sad face. It wasn't fair that someone had taken her aunt's trophy away. And it wasn't fair that someone had taken Zoe's special necklace.

I knew Mrs. Sinclair only wanted me to write about the personal side of the thefts, but surely I could also keep an eye out for clues? I wasn't about to go and accuse anyone of stealing anything. But if I was writing an article on the issue anyway, and interviewing the victims, then surely I had more insight into the mystery than anyone else.

I didn't know how I was going to do it, but I decided then and there that I was going to find Zoe's necklace and Mrs. Sinclair's trophy.

After class, we had another meeting of *Eden Press*. Ivy was running the meeting and we began our layout for the upcoming edition of the online paper. A couple of the Year 9 girls who were really good at online design had begun making a template for the new-look paper, which we hoped more people would be reading.

Two Year 8 girls were working together on the puzzle section—creating word searches and sudokus, as well as mazes and crosswords.

A girl named Sara was editing photos on the computer—photos she had taken of the recent music ensemble concert and the Seniors' debate team. I watched in awe as she zoomed in on the photos, editing them to make them brighter and clearer. She was like a magician with a wand. It was so cool.

I sat at a desk near Ivy and a few other writers working on their journalistic pieces, too.

"So, how's the article on the thefts going, Ella?" Ivy asked.

I saw Saskia glance up at us, then quickly look back down at her screen.

I was slightly surprised to see Saskia at the meeting. She'd missed the last meeting, saying she had to study for our upcoming streaming tests. She seemed to be taking that whole thing pretty seriously, even though all the teachers said it wasn't a big deal.

"Pretty good," I said. "I've got my interviews with the victims of the thefts and I'm going to add a piece about the headmistress that donated the House trophy that was stolen."

Ivy nodded. "Good work, Ella."

Saskia rolled her eyes.

"What are you working on, Sass?" Ivy asked her sister.

"It's top secret," Saskia said, as she minimized her open window.

"Well, as Editor, don't you think I should know what you are writing?" Ivy asked.

"Don't worry—I'll show it to you soon," Saskia chirped.

Ivy narrowed her eyes and smiled slightly.

"OK, I need someone to cover the athletics meet next week," Ivy said in a loud voice to everyone in the room. "Who has time?"

"I can!" Saskia jumped up.

"Really?" her sister asked. "You just said you're working on something else. And I know you've been really bogged down with studying for your testing. I don't want you overwhelming yourself."

"It's *fine*," Saskia laughed. "I've studied my head off—I don't think I need to study much more anyway."

"No more studying? That doesn't sound like you, Sass! Usually you study right up until the last minute," Ivy laughed.

Saskia flashed a bright smile and waved her hand in the air. "Oh, I'm prepared. And I'm sure I'll end up in the top stream anyway, so what's there left to stress about?"

Ivy shrugged, clearly confused. "OK, if you are happy with that, it'd be great if you could cover the meet."

"Done!" Saskia sang.

She sure was in a good mood today.

"OK, everyone, feel free to go when you need to," Ivy said, beginning to shut down her laptop. "Great work today, reporters!"

I watched Saskia as she continued to type on her computer. She seemed so much more bubbly today. I wondered why.

"And what are *you* looking at?"

I startled as Saskia caught me staring at her.

"Oh, nothing," I mumbled. "I was just thinking that you're in a good mood today."

"Well, why wouldn't I be? The sun is shining, I've got new ideas for *Eden Press* and I'm going to absolutely nail those streaming tests. What's not to love?"

"I guess," I said uncertainly.

As I finished packing up my things, Saskia shut down her computer and gathered her own belongings together. She flashed a smile at her sister and skipped out the door. Ivy looked at me with a confused expression. Then she simply shrugged and gathered her items together before following Saskia out of the room.

Chapter 11

From: <u>Ella</u>

Sent: Monday, 7:30 AM

To: <u>Olivia</u>

Subject: Weird, weird, WEIRD!

Hi Olivia!

Mum told me you went through to finals at the swim meet. That's awesome! What else has been happening? It's week three now, which means one thing: my class tests must be soon. They're just to stream us into our classes, but I'm a bit nervous about it all. Saskia reckons you can lose your scholarship if you don't do well in them. I don't know if that's true or not, but I hope I can do OK, especially in English.

Remember I told you about the stolen items at school? I'm investigating them for *Eden Press*. All the items have gone missing from the Year 7 dorm, except for one—a trophy from Mrs. Sinclair's office. But I can't work out why on earth anyone would want to steal that?! Mrs. Sinclair said it's not worth lots of money. What would someone do with a trophy?! It's really WEIRD.

Speaking of weird, I asked Violet to sit with us at dinner last night. She did, but then halfway through eating she went kind of pale and left. I just don't get that girl.

Email me!

Love, Ella

xx

PS. I STILL hear a clinking sound every night by my door. It's so creepy! I'm too scared to get out of bed and check it out. I need a ghost trap—can you invent one for me???

I loathe PE. PE is physical education, or sports class.
Don't get me wrong, I love gymnastics and dance and
I even got pretty good at soccer at the end of primary
school. Because I am so nimble and agile (that means
light on my feet), I was a pretty good goalie. But PE is
not my favorite subject. In primary school we'd have
to run laps around the field. Or do a thousand jumping
jacks. Or play tug-of-war, where the boys would get so
competitive that it would feel like our arms were getting
yanked out of their sockets.

I was sitting on the grass with Grace and Zoe. Two
other girls in our year, Annabelle and Ruby, had come
to sit with us too. Annabelle was the one who'd had her
watch stolen from her room. I'd already interviewed
her about it. We sat in a circle on the field, waiting
for our PE teacher to arrive. I stretched out my legs
and felt the warm summer sun beating down on me. I
rolled down my socks as far as they would go to try to
avoid getting a sock tan line. So unsightly, as Nanna
Kate would say!

We all wore matching sports uniforms, which consisted of a teal T-shirt with a royal-blue collar. It also had royal-blue cuffs at the shoulders and our initials were embroidered onto the sleeve. The T-shirt showed the Eden crest, which had the school motto printed in Latin underneath. "*In Meliora Contende*," I whispered.

We also wore royal-blue shorts and white socks with white sneakers. For Christmas, I had received new purple sneakers with bright-blue laces. They had a neon-blue lightning bolt up the side and Dad said they would make me run extra fast. But then I found out Eden only allows *white* sneakers, which is very boring and not very expressive. So I have to save my cool sneakers for weekends. We also all wore matching royal-blue caps with our ponytails pulled through the hole in the back. So much matchy-matchy at this school. It really does make it tough for a girl to express her fashion sense.

"Can't we just sit here in the sun all day?" Grace said, dreamily. "I don't want to get up and *run*."

"Maybe PE is different in high school," Zoe suggested.

"I don't think so," Annabelle laughed, flicking her long, black ponytail over her shoulder. "Haven't you heard about Coach Bright?"

"What about her—"

"EVERYBODY UP!" a voice boomed from behind us. This was followed by what can only be described as excessive whistle use.

A woman ran onto the field. She wore sports shorts, a T-shirt and long, white socks. Around her head was a fluorescent-pink sweatband, and a silver whistle was clenched between her teeth. Her frizzy blond hair curled out of the top of her sweatband and she looked a bit like Mum did that time she and Dad dressed up for an 80s theme party. I remember Mum yelling, "The 80s are BACK!" and looking at Coach Bright, I guess she was right.

She jumped from foot to foot while intermittently blowing her whistle and yelling, "Up! Up! Up!"

We fumbled about, trying to get to our feet as quickly as possible.

"Gather around," she yelled, which was odd because

we were already standing pretty close to her. "Right, follow me!"

And with that, she bolted off up the grass, waving for us to follow.

We were all too shocked to complain and ran after her like a clumsy pack of toddlers. She ran us around the field four times (and the Eden field is WAY bigger than our primary school field). When we all got back to our starting places, we were hunched over, puffing and trying to catch our breath.

"You are all so unfit!" Coach Bright boomed. "You are meant to be my young, spritely Year 7 girls! Why so sluggish? Too many midnight feasts already?"

Grace's face went bright red.

"Follow my stretches!" Coach Bright cried.

We all stretched out our arms, necks and legs, before collapsing into a heap on the grass.

"When will this be over?" Annabelle moaned.

"Over?" Coach Bright yelled, overhearing Annabelle. "Why, we've only just begun! Now the FUN starts! We're going to play a game."

Coach Bright dragged over a big, net bag filled with balls.

I like plenty of types of balls—soccer balls, gumballs, Cinderella's ball, crystal balls, disco balls, I could go on and on. But there's one ball I *really* despise and it's . . .

"DODGEBALL!" yelled Coach Bright.

I slapped my forehead.

"OK, grab a bib. Girls on this side, you are the red team. And girls on this side, you are the white team. I'll line up the balls in the center of the field. Everyone go to their team sides, and when I blow the whistle, you run in and get a ball. Remember, you can only hit people with the ball on the legs. If you get hit, you're out!"

We all took our places. I had Grace, Zoe, Annabelle and Ruby on my side, as well as some other girls from my class. I could see Saskia, Portia and Mercedes on the opposing team. Portia and Mercedes looked most unimpressed, but Saskia bounced around excitedly, ready to compete. I could also see Violet standing toward the back of their team.

"On your mark, get set . . ." Coach Bright blew

forcefully through her whistle as everyone ran into the center to get a ball.

As soon as I reached the center, balls started flying around all over the place. I ducked and dodged and jumped to keep out of the way. In my peripheral vision, I saw a ball smack into Zoe's thigh.

"Ow!" she complained, rubbing her leg as she walked to the sideline.

I threw my ball and it rolled into Mercedes' ankle as she stood still, unmoving.

"Oh, I'm out, how terrible," she said sarcastically.

The numbers slowly began to dwindle as more and more people got hit with a ball. As much as I don't like dodgeball, I had to admit, I was doing pretty well!

Soon there were only four of us left. Annabelle and me versus Saskia and Portia.

Saskia threw the ball hard and fast. Annabelle dodged it, but then lost her footing and fell over. While she was on the ground, Portia gently rolled the ball into her legs.

"You're out!" Portia yelled.

Annabelle got up and walked off the field. "Go, Ella!" she yelled. I was the last one left.

I heard Saskia yelling tactics to Portia to get me out. "Portia, go left! Let's attack, one after the other! Throw harder!"

Saskia hurled the ball toward my knees. I did a big jump over it and landed awkwardly on my ankle. It didn't hurt, but it did cause me to lose my balance and my body came down into a crouch.

Right at that moment, I saw Portia's arm whip back and release.

BANG.

Everything went black for a second. I stumbled backward, falling onto my bottom as a hot pain surged through my eye.

"Oh, Ella, I'm so sorry!" Portia squealed, as she came running over. "I was aiming for your legs—I didn't expect you to be down!"

Pain throbbed in my eye.

"OK, clear the way," Coach Bright said, tutting as she waded through the crowd that had gathered around me. "Let me have a little look."

She gently pulled my hand away from my eye. "You might have a bit of a black eye there, Ella," she said. "But I loved how you put your body on the line!"

I didn't love it.

"Violet, can you please take Ella down to the sick bay to get some ice?"

Violet shuffled over from the back of the crowd and gently took my arm. "Come on, Ella," she whispered, as she helped me up. Everyone was staring at me and I felt mortified. Which means extremely embarrassed.

"Everyone else, let's get ready for ROUND TWO!" Coach Bright hollered. Everyone groaned.

Violet continued to loosely hold my arm as we walked off the field and onto the path that wound its way through the school.

"I've never been to the sick bay. Do you know the way?" I asked.

"Yes," she said flatly.

We walked in silence until we arrived at a little building down by the dormitories. Violet held the door for me as we walked inside. Everything looked clean and sanitary. White walls. White floor. White cabinets. There was the unmistakable smell of antiseptic in the air. The reception room at the front of the office was empty except for a desk and some chairs scattered around the room. I could see smaller rooms off the reception area and, as I peeked inside, I spied long hospital beds with crisp, white linen.

There was a little bell on the desk, which Violet rang. The school nurse came bundling out of one of the side rooms, her hands full of rolled-up bandages. When she saw Violet, she hurriedly dropped the bandages onto the empty desk.

"Violet, are you OK? Do you need—" the nurse began as she ran up to Violet.

"It's not me," Violet interrupted forcefully. "It's Ella. She took a ball to the eye."

The nurse turned to me. "Oh, sorry, Ella, I thought you were here with Violet."

Why would Violet need the nurse?

"Let's get some ice on that," she said, ushering me

into a chair. Violet sat next to me.

As the nurse went over to get the ice, Violet said, "I hope you're OK."

"Thanks. How does the nurse know you already?" I asked.

Violet's cheeks flushed pink. "I've been down for a headache before," she said quickly.

We sat silently.

The nurse came back and gently pried my hand from my face. She carefully looked into my eye with a little light before handing me the ice pack.

"I don't think there's any need to be concerned about damage to your eye, Ella," she said chirpily. "It's just a bruise and it should heal pretty quickly. You might get some darker bruising over the next few days, but if you are in any way worried, please don't hesitate to come back. Now, I'll need to fill out an Incident Report, so just wait here with the ice on it. Violet, you can go back to class."

Violet nodded and then turned to me. "You'll be OK," she said, smiling lightly.

I smiled back.

"I'll see you later this afternoon, Violet," the nurse called out over her shoulder.

Violet's smile vanished and she fiddled with her sports cap.

"Why are—" I began.

"See you later, Ella," Violet interrupted as she hurriedly opened the door and jogged off into the sunshine.

Chapter 12

I remember when Max, Olivia and I would have sleepovers at Nanna Kate's. She has a special room in her house just for us—it has two single beds and we put a blow-up mattress in between. There used to be a crib in her room, but then Max got too old for that, so now he sleeps on the blow-up mattress on the floor. We always have the best time at Nanna Kate's sleepovers. She bakes with us and even lets us crack all the eggs. One time, she made us a treasure map and we had to go all around the house, following her clues, until we got to the treasure at the end, which was chocolate, of course.

She is also really good at helping us to make surprises for Mum and Dad, without them knowing. One year, right before Mother's Day, we decided we wanted to grow Mum some flowers in a pot. We bought the seeds with our own pocket money the day before, and we took them to Nanna Kate's because she has lots of pots of all different colors and sizes.

When we showed Nanna Kate the seeds, she frowned and said she wasn't sure if the seeds would grow into full-sized flowers overnight. Max threw a tantrum and Olivia cried—we really wanted to have the flowers ready for Mum because nobody wants a pot of dirt as a present. Then Nanna Kate told us that plants need love, just like people, so perhaps if we talked to our seeds, played them music and then made a special wish, they might just grow.

So we decorated the pot with paint and filled it with dirt. We gave each seed a kiss and made a wish before pushing it into the soil and patting it down with our fingers. Then we sprinkled water on top of the soil and put it in the sunshine, while we sang sweet songs to the seeds.

The next morning, we raced outside to see if our flowers had magically grown. And to our delight, they had sprung up into full blooms of pink, white and purple. Nanna Kate said they were pansies. They looked beautiful and we knew Mum would just love them, which she did, of course, and pansies became my most favorite flower in the whole wide world.

I only noticed this past summer that Mr. Rodriguez, who lives next door to Nanna Kate, grows many pots of pansies and has them all over his courtyard.

I decided maybe pansies weren't so magical after all.

It's funny how things can change when you look back on them. It's like rewatching a movie from when you were little and realizing you missed the point the whole time. I guess that's just part of growing up.

"Ella?"

"Sorry, what was the question?" I asked, embarrassed. I'd been gazing at the colorful flower box of pansies which hung outside the window.

"Move over to that group there with Saskia, Ruby, Violet and Annabelle," Miss Tempest said, irritated.

I picked up my laptop and carried it over to the other table. I loved English class, but was not too keen on being in a group with Saskia. The classroom had lots of different learning spaces to use for group work. There were little tables low to the ground or higher ones with tall stools. There were beanbags in the corner, or you could even sit at desks with whiteboard surfaces, so you could write your ideas straight onto the table with an erasable marker.

I sat down and smiled at the other girls in my group. Saskia sat up straight, with her fingers poised over her keyboard.

"Would you like me to be the scribe?" she asked.

Everyone shrugged, then agreed.

"So, the task states that we need to come up with a descriptive passage about this image," she said, turning her laptop so that we could all see the screen.

The image showed a rusty gate, flanked by a low, brick wall. Through the gate you could see a winding path of cobblestones, leading into a misty darkness. Bare-limbed trees peppered the scene, with long, spindly fingers reaching out over the path.

"Why don't we start with a brainstorm of words and phrases that we think of when we look at it?" I said.

The others nodded in agreement. Except Saskia.

"Or . . ." she said as she flicked her laptop back around to face her. She navigated with the cursor, clicked some files and then turned the screen back around.

"Voilà!" she declared.

We all leaned in to look at her screen. She had opened a document with a full-page description on it. It was entitled "The Haunted Lake."

"What's that?" Annabelle asked.

"It's a descriptive passage I wrote last year. I worked on it with my tutor and it's brilliant," Saskia smiled. "I have a whole heap of these things and I can pull them out whenever there's a relevant topic. And I *always* get perfect marks when I hand them in!"

Ruby frowned. "But this task isn't even about a haunted lake."

"But look at the *language*," Saskia protested. "It's

all about ominous rising mist, the shriek of the owl, the foreboding glow of the lamplight . . ."

"There's no lamplight," Annabelle interjected.

"It doesn't matter! You're missing the point. What I'm saying is that with a couple of quick clicks, we can change this to fit the picture and we'll have an instant winner!" Saskia said breathlessly.

The group looked around at each other with puzzled expressions.

"But what's the point in just copying your tutor's old work? Then we won't actually get to *do* anything," Ruby said.

"Yeah, I want to write it ourselves," Annabelle added.

Violet nodded meekly in agreement.

"Me, too," I shrugged.

"The *point*," Saskia said, exasperated, "is to get the best mark. This is an absolute guarantee we'll get the best mark in the class," she said, with eyebrows raised.

"I don't want the best mark if it's not our work," I said flatly.

Saskia's face turned from hopeful to angry. "I can't work with you people," she said, slapping her laptop shut and standing up. "I'm going to another group."

I looked at the others in my group as Saskia stormed off. Then we all burst out laughing.

"Quiet, please, and get on with your work," Miss Tempest scolded from up at the front.

We smothered our giggles and I opened my laptop. The screen lit up and I clicked on a new, blank document. Annabelle pulled up the image and we began to brainstorm the words and emotions we felt when we looked at the image.

Haunting.

Eerie.

Mystical.

Ominous.

Sinister.

Grim.

By the time we finished, we had collected two whole pages of words, phrases and descriptions. We'd begun pulling all the ideas together to make a descriptive passage, when the bell pierced through the air, marking the end of the school day. We agreed to meet later in the dorm study room to finish the task for homework.

I gathered up my laptop and books and carried them in a small pile in my arms. Grace and Zoe ran up to me as we left the classroom.

"Let's go via the dining hall and grab afternoon tea," Zoe said.

Grace and I agreed as we headed down the path, back toward the dorms and the dining hall. When we got to the dining hall, there were piles of muffins sitting in wicker baskets. Some students were eating inside and others were taking them outside to sit in the afternoon sun. We decided to take ours outside and sit on the grass.

I looked around and saw a few girls walking up the path in their sports gear, holding softball bats. Others carried musical instrument cases as they headed off to afternoon band and music rehearsals. Some girls were sitting in groups on the grass, reading books, chatting or even sleeping in the afternoon sunshine.

"Your eye is looking better already," Zoe said.

I raised my hand to where the ball had hit me in PE. It hadn't bruised badly at all, thankfully.

"So, how's your investigation of the thefts going, Ella?" Grace asked, in between bites of her muffin.

"I haven't gotten very far yet," I conceded, as I rescued a crumb from the corner of my mouth with my tongue.

"Got any theories?" Zoe asked.

"Well," I said slowly, pulling out my notebook. "I have a hunch that these robberies are happening at night. All of them have been in the dorm except one, and that one was definitely not during school hours because Mrs. Sinclair's office was empty."

Grace and Zoe nodded as they peered over my notes.

"I also think," I continued, "that it's a Year 7 student. Since all the thefts have been on our floor, except for one, I think it's obvious that it was probably easiest to access for a girl in our year."

"So, what now?" Grace asked.

I bit my lip and looked up at the tree above me.

Its green and yellow leaves blew gently in the summer breeze. I breathed in the sweet scent of jasmine as I thought.

"Maybe I could do some surveillance," I said. "That means high-tech spying," I added.

Zoe laughed. "We *know*, Ella. Anyway, how are you going to do that?"

"What if I set up my laptop on the hall table at the end of the Year 7 dorm hallway? If I turn the computer's camera on, I can film the hallway overnight. It will show if anyone from Year 7 gets up in the night!"

"What if they're going to the bathroom?" Grace said, with one eyebrow raised.

"I'll set it up facing the stairs—if anyone is going to the bathroom they won't come up as far as my laptop. This will *only* show girls who are leaving the floor!" I declared.

Zoe and Grace looked at each other and shrugged.

"It's a long shot," Grace said doubtfully.

"Worth a try," Zoe said.

I knew it was a long shot. The thefts hadn't been

taking place every single night. And if the theft was within a Year 7 dorm room, I wouldn't catch it on camera. But now that the culprit had already broken into Mrs. Sinclair's office, I had a feeling she would try her luck in other places around the school, too. I knew it could work.

It had to work.

Chapter 13

We tiptoed up the carpeted hallway, being careful to keep close to the wall where the floorboards creaked less. I used the soft glow of my book light to illuminate a path in front of us. The founding headmistresses glared down from their portraits disapprovingly.

As we neared the top of the staircase, Zoe signaled to me and Grace to gather in close.

"OK, so we'll set up the computer here," she said, gesturing to the small, wooden table with a large, blue vase on top of it.

"We can use the vase to hide the laptop, so it's not so

obvious," Grace whispered.

We nodded in agreement.

It was unlikely anyone was going to see the computer. It was a dark night and other than a sliver of light from the moon, the hallway was a cool, murky blue.

Zoe plugged the laptop into a socket behind the hall table and flipped open the lid. She switched the power button on.

DING!

The computer sang a triumphant sound as it powered up. We all madly fumbled to smother the speaker, our eyes wildly darting down the stairs in case Ms. Montgomery was patrolling.

Zoe muted the sound on the laptop and began clicking around the screen. Zoe is a complete computer whiz. She is really good at coding and making movies on the computer. She knew exactly what she was doing.

Her long, thin fingers danced across the keyboard as she opened and closed programs, adjusted the light and set the camera up for a long night of filming.

"This program I've downloaded is especially for surveillance," she said quietly, as she tapped the keys. "It will allow us to film the whole night, but we can play it back tomorrow in super speed. It will also indicate at which points in the video there is movement or sound."

Grace and I nodded.

Zoe made one last tweak to the placement of the laptop before whispering, "Done!"

Suddenly, we heard a door click shut downstairs.

We looked at each other with wild eyes and quickly bundled ourselves back up the hallway, running on our tiptoes. We dashed in through our dorm room door, smothering our giggles as we went. We each dived into our beds, trying not to wake Violet, who was gently snoring with her face to the wall.

"We did it!" I whispered excitedly.

"Let's just hope it was worth it, and Ms. Montgomery doesn't find the laptop," Zoe said nervously.

"It's well hidden, don't worry," Grace said. "And I've set my alarm for sunrise so we can go and grab it before anyone else is up."

The air grew quiet.

As I lay there, I heard Grace and Zoe's breaths slow down, until they were both breathing in a sleepy rhythm. But I was too excited to sleep. What if we caught the thief on camera? I could do an exposé in *Eden Press*. That's a special article that reveals a big scandal. I'd get Junior Journalist for sure and Zoe would get her necklace back. I sighed as my eyes began to get heavier. And I fell asleep with my fingers crossed.

I slid my tray along the counter and shuffled slowly up the line. I held up my plate for toast and the serving lady behind the counter plopped a spoonful of scrambled eggs on top. I also nodded eagerly for some grilled tomato and avocado on the side.

I pushed my tray along to the end of the serving counter and picked up my knife and fork. Grace and Zoe followed behind me as we hunted for a seat in the dining hall. There was a space down at the end of one of the long tables, so we went over and sat down there.

Grace's long, thick, dark hair was loose and damp from her shower that morning. She was still air-drying it and hadn't pulled it back into her signature French braid. During school hours, we weren't allowed to wear our hair down, but before and after school hours, on weekends and in the dorms, it was OK to leave it loose. She tucked a segment behind her ear and looked up with her cat-green eyes.

"So, when are we going to check our surveillance video?" she asked excitedly.

"Shh!" Zoe hissed. "Keep your voice down!"

"Let's do it after breakfast. We've got a good hour before class starts, so we can look over it back in the dorm," I said.

I dusted off a bit of toast which had crumbled onto my school dress.

Zoe spooned some cereal into her mouth. Her short, jet-black hair hung messily over her face, as she hadn't had time to brush it yet. "I've got the laptop in our room, ready."

I nodded excitedly.

"Can we join?" a voice chirped from behind us.

Saskia, Portia and Mercedes stood with their trays of breakfast, looking for a seat.

"Sure thing!" Grace said, making room on the bench for the others.

The three of them plonked themselves down and began to eat. Saskia already looked completely neat and tidy, all ready for school. Her blond hair was pulled up into a high ponytail with a white ribbon wound around the elastic. Her blue eyes shone.

"Attention, everyone," Ms. Montgomery said into a microphone from up at the front of the hall.

The chatter in the dining hall died down.

"I have a few announcements this Wednesday morning, before you all get ready for the day, so please listen carefully."

There was a din of clinks as everyone put down their cutlery, ready to listen.

"First, Year 10, remember you have your geography field trip to the wetlands next week. We have emailed your parents a permission form, but please do remind them to send it back if they haven't already. Year 7, you will have your testing day for class streaming this Friday. We will begin with English at 9:00 a.m. and then you will have a break before math in the afternoon. These are the only two subjects which will be streamed this year."

There was a murmur of dread among all the Year 7 girls. I swallowed hard. Friday was only two days away. I'd been so focused on my newspaper article that I'd barely studied for the tests at all.

Ms. Montgomery gestured for silence then continued. "Mr. Matthews, the school handyman, is coming tomorrow to do some maintenance. He will be repairing the lock on the shower door in the Year 9 dormitory, fixing some things in Mrs. Sinclair's office and installing an extra set of shelves in the common room. If you see any other things around the dormitories that need attention, please tell me today so I can add them to his list. That is all."

Ms. Montgomery sat down at the teachers' table

by herself, away from the other teachers who were chatting over their breakfasts. She took a long, deep sip of her coffee and closed her eyes momentarily as she swallowed. Then she looked back down at the newspaper that was open in front of her and resumed reading.

"Ready for Friday's testing?" Saskia asked.

I looked away from Ms. Montgomery.

"Ugh," Grace huffed. "I hate tests."

"Well, I don't!" Saskia laughed. "I can't wait to do them. I'm going to top the year, I can just feel it!"

Zoe rolled her eyes.

"Come on," I urged Zoe and Grace. "We've got to get back to the dorm."

"What's the rush?" Portia asked.

"Yeah, what are you three up to?" Saskia said, narrowing her eyes.

"Oh, nothing. Just need to get ready for school," I said hurriedly, pointing to my messy bun, which was bundled on top of my head.

Grace and Zoe jumped up with their trays and

shuffled after me. I looked back over my shoulder and saw Saskia purse her lips.

We needed to be very careful. She was definitely suspicious.

Chapter 14

Grace closed our bedroom door and ran back over to my bed. She jumped on, rocking me and Zoe as we crowded around the laptop.

"Quick, let's see before Violet gets back from breakfast," said Grace.

Zoe held the computer in her lap and began navigating around the screen. She opened the file with the overnight footage.

The image on the screen was dark and grainy.

"Will we be able to see anything?" I asked, worried.

"Yes, just let me pump the resolution up a bit," she

said, her fingers clacking the keys.

We watched as she switched the video on. Nothing appeared to happen; the video just showed the quiet stairwell in the darkness.

"If you look along here," Zoe said, pointing to a bar running along the bottom of the screen, "it will show us at what points in the night movement or sound occurred. See here, at 10:07 p.m., we get something."

I leaned in, holding my breath.

Zoe flicked the cursor along the bar to 10:07 p.m. and turned up the sound. Nothing came onto the screen, but we did hear the unmistakable sound of the bathroom door opening and squeaking closed.

"Just someone going for a visit," Grace said, disappointed.

I giggled.

"What about there?" I asked, pointing to a marker further along. It was at 10:35 p.m.

Zoe pulled up the footage and we saw movement on the staircase. Ms. Montgomery glided up the stairs and turned down the hallway. She was doing her final checks on everyone before going to bed herself, we figured. We saw her walk back down the hall again about two minutes later, and on down the stairs.

"Ugh!" I huffed, frustrated.

Zoe looked along the bar and pointed to another portion of sound activity. She pumped up the volume again.

Clink.

Clink.

Clink.

We all looked at each other, confused.

The sounds got louder. But there was nothing onscreen.

Clink.

Clink.

The sound of the gentle clinking grew so loud, whatever was making it was clearly right next to the laptop. But there was still nothing on the screen!

Zoe scrunched up her nose. Grace's eyes were wide.

BANG!

We all jumped as a loud *bang* echoed out of the

computer. We leaned in and saw the blue vase gently rolling on its side.

"The vase *was* knocked over this morning!" Grace said.

"What knocked it over?" I asked in a shaky voice.

"You don't think Saskia was right, do you?" Zoe asked. "I mean, about the ghost of Ms. Montgomery's fiancé?"

Grace let out a nervous laugh. "As if," she said. But she didn't sound so sure.

"Look, there's some more activity at 2:02 a.m.," I said, keen to get away from the ghost question.

Zoe pulled the cursor along and brought up the footage. We could hear light footsteps padding up the hallway. Suddenly, there was a figure standing right in front of the screen. It was hard to tell who it was because her back was turned to the screen and it was grainy and dark. But she had a light coat on. Like she was going outside.

"Who is it?" Grace hissed, leaning in closer and squinting at the screen.

"She's not tall," Zoe remarked, turning her head to one side.

The figure looked left and right, then started tiptoeing down the stairs.

"Look, she has shoes on!" I exclaimed. "She's clearly going *out*."

We still couldn't tell who it was.

"Well, whatever goes out, must come back in," Grace shrugged. "Scan ahead for when she comes back."

We looked at the computer screen and saw that the next flurry of activity was around ten minutes later.

The figure padded back up the stairs, looking left to right again as she went. When she got to the top of the stairs, she looked right square in the direction of the computer camera.

She was small.

Her skin was pale in the moonlight.

She had a little face.

And big round glasses.

We all gasped.

It was Violet.

Chapter 15

✕ —

From: <u>Ella</u>

Sent: Wednesday, 12:15 PM

To: <u>Olivia</u>

Subject: What do I do??!!!

Hi Olivia,

You'll never believe what's going on here. I think we caught the Eden Thief. It's Violet. You know, the girl in my room who is really quiet and weird? Yeah, well, we saw her sneaking out at 2:00 a.m.

I don't know what to do. I've got the evidence on

video—do I show Mrs. Sinclair? But she specifically told me not to accuse people. Do I confront Violet? What will she do? I'm so confused.

I also think we caught a ghost on camera, but that's another story.

Thanks for your email. That story about you and your friends—LOL! I can't believe you used Max and Bob to create a diversion while you snuck into the kitchen to take the cookies . . .

Wait a second! Oh my gosh, I've just had an epiphany! Just like in *Millie Mysteries*! Gotta go—will explain everything later!!!

Love, Ella

xx

I pushed the "send" button and slapped my laptop shut. Grabbing it, I ran out of the dorm study room and out onto Centenary Lawn, where Grace and Zoe were having lunch in the sun. Grace's long, tanned legs were stretched out in front of her and Zoe's were tucked up underneath her. Zoe had chosen a sandwich from the dining hall and Grace had a wrap. I bolted over to them and sat down, nearly knocking over their drinks.

"Whoa, slow down, Ella!" Grace laughed.

"No time! I've worked it out!" I blurted.

"Worked what out?" asked Zoe.

I put my laptop down and pulled my notebook and pen out of my bag, hurriedly flicking through the pages of notes I'd written on the dorm thefts. I found the section of notes from when I'd met with Mrs. Sinclair.

"Here," I said, circling something I'd written.

Zoe and Grace leaned in to look. I'd circled the words "Filing cabinet key lost."

"So what?" said Grace.

"Mrs. Sinclair lost her filing cabinet key right after her office was burgled," I explained. "Bit of a coincidence, isn't it?"

Zoe frowned.

"Olivia emailed me and told me this funny story about how she and her friends got Bob and Max to create a diversion so that they could sneak into the kitchen and steal cookies from the pantry," I said breathlessly.

"What's that got to do with anything?" Grace said.

"That's when it hit me! It's a *diversion*!" I said, wide-eyed.

"Like, a distraction?" Zoe asked.

"Exactly!"

"The thief is stealing cookies?" Grace asked.

"No!" I laughed. "The thefts are a diversion. What have we all been concentrating on since the items have gone missing?"

"Well . . . the missing stuff, I guess?" Grace shrugged.

"Yes. The missing necklace, the watch, the scarf and then the trophy. Those all seemed like valuable things," I said. "But what if they were stolen to cover up the thing that the thief *really* wanted?"

"Which is . . ." Zoe asked.

"Mrs. Sinclair's key! She didn't lose it—it was taken! But when she saw that the window was open and the trophy gone, she thought it was because the thief *wanted* the trophy. But the thief didn't want the trophy.

She wanted something in the filing cabinet!"

"Like what?" Grace asked.

"I have no idea," I said. "But I do know that the thief will be back tonight."

"Why tonight?" Zoe asked.

"Because of the announcements this morning! Remember what's happening tomorrow?" I prompted.

"Tacos?" Grace asked.

"No! The handyman is coming to fix Mrs. Sinclair's filing cabinet. Whatever was taken will need to be returned by tonight, otherwise Mrs. Sinclair will know what the thief was *really* interested in!"

Zoe looked doubtful. "Are you sure, Ella? That seems like a pretty elaborate plan."

"But it makes *sense*," I insisted. "And now that we know who the thief is, all we have to do is catch her in the act tonight."

"You still think it's Violet?" Zoe asked.

"I know it's Violet. But I don't know why. We need to catch her in Mrs. Sinclair's office and then we can confront her."

Zoe and Grace looked at me silently.

"You know," Grace said, "if you're wrong and we're caught, we could get in a whole heap of trouble. We're not even allowed out of our dorm rooms at night, let alone out of the house."

"I'm not wrong," I insisted. "I can feel it in my bones. This is right. Are you with me or not?"

Grace sucked in a sharp breath. Zoe bit her lower lip.

"OK, I'm in." Grace put her hand out into the middle of the circle.

"Me, too. But only because you've been my best friend since we were, like, five," Zoe said, putting her hand on top of Grace's.

I put my hand on top of their hands and smiled.

"Let's do this."

Chapter 16

When my Nanna Kate was younger, she traveled with her best friend all around the world. She told me that when they were in France, they went to a very famous museum to look at a display of rare gems and minerals. They were extremely valuable and heavily guarded. She liked them because they shone so brightly in the afternoon sun. She said it was like looking into the eyes of the moon. All types of people came to see the display—there were older people whose tired eyes were reignited by the dazzling display, there were students and parents and even a very young girl, maybe four years of age, who kept pointing at the shiny rocks with her eyebrows raised. Nanna Kate said the little girl dropped her doll and she picked it up for her and told her the doll's eyes were as sparkly as the gems on display, which the little girl laughed about. But her mother scolded the girl for talking to strangers.

Nanna Kate said they were just about to leave when an alarm sounded and panic ensued. Two of the most valuable gems were gone from the display—despite the security guards, someone had stolen them. The security doors were closed and everyone was asked to show their bags. As the police and guards checked Nanna Kate's bag, she saw the little girl and her mother leaving, the mother's bag having already been checked. That's when Nanna Kate realized. She told the guard, and, sure enough, they found the missing gems hidden in the head of the little girl's doll, stuck behind the glass eyes so they didn't rattle. That's why the doll's eyes had sparkled so much. The mother had planned the whole thing—nobody would ever have suspected that the thief was a four-year-old child, you see.

And so, Nanna Kate always says, appearances can be deceiving.

I thought about this story as Grace, Zoe and I got ready to crack open this mystery. It was lights-out in the dorm and Violet was in her bed, fast asleep. We quietly crawled out of our beds and pushed our pillows and some clothes under our blankets, to make it look like we were still sleeping. Violet couldn't know we weren't there, otherwise she might be suspicious and not try to sneak out herself.

Zoe, Grace and I only spoke in hand movements.

We slipped on our sweatshirts—even though it was a summer night, we wanted our hoods up to obscure our faces. And we made sure we were wearing dark colors all over our bodies, so we could sneak around in the night without being seen.

I quietly pulled on my sneakers, which are good for sneaking. Grace slipped her backpack over her shoulder—it had her digital camera in it, so we could take a photo as evidence. And we'd also packed a flashlight and some rope. I don't know why we packed rope, really, but the spies in movies always seem to have rope, so we thought we'd better bring some just in case.

I slid my hood up over my head and gestured to Grace and Zoe to move toward the door.

Zoe opened the door, which creaked loudly.

We whipped around to check that Violet was still asleep.

She was. Phew!

We snuck out into the hallway and tiptoed up the carpet. Every time we heard even the faintest noise, we'd plaster our bodies against the cool wall, trying to remain hidden.

Grace led the way down the stairs and toward the big front doors of the dormitory. This was going to be tricky. The doors were heavy and made a loud clunking sound when they closed, so we had to be extra careful.

Grace held the door while Zoe and I bundled out, then slipped out after us. She kept the door open and looked down at her watch.

"Three, two, one," she mouthed.

Right on "one," the clock in the hallway chimed

10:00 p.m. and she closed the door, using the chimes of the clock to muffle the *clunk* the door made.

We nodded at each other. Our plan was going flawlessly.

We padded up the path, winding our way back into the main part of the school. Everything looked so different at night. The tall, old-fashioned buildings looked creepy under the moonlight and I half expected bats to come swooping down from the steeple.

But they didn't. Of course.

We walked all the way up to the administration block, and only stopped once we were outside the foyer of the office, right under a window. Zoe gave me a boost up and I pushed the window open. I knew the window would be unlocked because we had set it up earlier that afternoon.

Grace and I had gone up to the office and, while Grace distracted the secretary by asking for some forms she said she needed, I had quietly unlatched the window from the inside.

So it was ready and waiting for us now.

I slid my body through the open window and then helped Zoe and Grace lift themselves up and over. We were in.

We crept behind the secretary's counter and along the short corridor to Mrs. Sinclair's office. Her door was shut. I wondered for a panicked moment if it was locked—that would spoil our entire plan!

I jiggled the doorknob and was relieved when the door creaked open.

Inside, Mrs. Sinclair's office was dark and cold.

I had a sudden sense of guilt. It felt like we were betraying Mrs. Sinclair's trust and invading her privacy. My cheeks flushed red with uncertainty. But I wanted to get her trophy back. And Zoe's necklace. And find out exactly what Violet was up to.

"OK, what now?" Zoe whispered.

"Now, we wait," I said solemnly.

We ducked down beside Mrs. Sinclair's desk. Grace turned her flashlight on, but I told her to switch it off— if Violet saw the light through the window of the office, she wasn't going to come in.

Grace unzipped her backpack and pulled out her digital camera, ready to snap a photo when the culprit arrived. She also pulled out a pack of marshmallows.

"Grace! That's so unprofessional!" I complained.

"What? We need energy for a stakeout. This could be a long night!"

I shook my head and, even though I disapproved, I took a marshmallow and ate it.

"What's going to happen to Violet when we expose her?" Zoe asked softly.

I hadn't really thought about that. I had a sudden feeling of remorse. That means deep regret.

"What if she gets expelled?" Grace asked.

I shrugged awkwardly. "But she can't just get away with it either," I reminded them, pushing away my guilty feelings.

We sat in silence, thinking about the whole situation.

I leaned against the wall and a wave of tiredness suddenly took over my whole body.

"Maybe we should take turns staying awake," Zoe suggested.

"I'll go first," Grace offered.

Zoe and I leaned on each other and closed our eyes. I wanted to stay awake, but the pull of sleep was just too strong. I felt myself drifting . . . swaying . . . falling.

Suddenly, a noise outside startled us all.

"Grace, did you fall asleep?" I hissed accusingly.

Grace shrugged guiltily.

"There's someone outside!" I whispered.

There was another *clang*—someone was fiddling with the window! Grace, Zoe and I ducked down behind Mrs. Sinclair's desk, completely out of sight.

Then Violet appeared in the window—it was definitely the shape of a young girl, all in black, with a small backpack hugging her body. She wore a black sweatshirt with the hood pulled tightly over her face. I couldn't see her glasses, but I knew it was her.

She slithered in, like a snake slithers into its burrow, and landed on the floor with a *thud*.

I looked at Grace and Zoe and made a hand movement that meant "ready for our plan?" They both gave a thumbs-up. When Zoe gave the signal, I was to jump up and hit the lights so Grace could snap a photo of Violet, frozen in the act.

Violet stalked across the office like a cat. She was light on her feet and her sleek legs made soundless movements. She slinked over to the filing cabinet. When she was standing in front of it, she reached into her sweatshirt pocket and pulled out a silver key. The moonlight bounced off the metal.

She pulled her backpack around to her front and very slowly unzipped it, careful not to make a sound. Then she pulled something out of her bag—something I couldn't quite make out in the dark. But it looked like a rolled-up cylinder of paper. I craned my neck for a better view.

She unrolled the paper, which now looked more like a manila folder full of papers, and smoothed them out flat on top of the cabinet. Then she slipped the key into the lock.

The drawer rolled open, smooth on its gliders.

Zoe made the hand movement.

I leapt up and hit the lights.

Grace took a photo.

Violet whipped around, her mouth agape and her eyebrows raised in shock and fear.

We all gasped in unison.

Because it wasn't Violet at all.

Chapter 17

We were flabbergasted (that means completely shocked and astonished).

It took me a minute to process who I was looking at. Her face had turned pale. Her blue eyes shone with the hint of tears. Her blond hair peeked out from the sides of her hood.

"Saskia?" I breathed.

"Wh—what are you doing here?" she cried in a wavering voice.

Grace and Zoe stood as still as statues.

"We are catching the Eden Thief," Grace said, after

a moment's silence. "Which appears to be *you*."

Saskia tried to say something, moving her mouth into the shape of words, but nothing came out. I could tell she was about to deny it, but then she looked down at her black clothing, her backpack and the folder of paper in her hands and closed her mouth again. Her shoulders slumped in resignation. There was no point arguing. She was caught red-handed.

She dropped the manila folder onto the carpet and pages spilled out onto the floor. Then she covered her face with both hands and began to sob. Her shoulders shook and the muffled sound of her cries hung in the air.

Grace, Zoe and I didn't move. What could we do? But as Saskia's sobs grew louder, I couldn't help but lunge forward and wrap my arms around her shoulders. She sank into my hug and sobbed louder.

She was like a different person. A topsy-turvy, upside-down Saskia. She wasn't confident and proud, but small and fragile. It was like the time Max went into the hospital with a really bad fever. For a while we didn't know what was wrong with him. And when we were in the waiting room, I saw a tear trickle down my dad's cheek. It made me feel scared and unsettled— this wasn't my fortress of a dad, this was a topsy-turvy, upside-down dad. A dad who got scared and sad, just like kids do.

And that's what it was like seeing Saskia shaking and shuddering with sadness.

"I didn't mean to . . ." she bawled. "I never meant to hurt anyone. I was going to return everything!"

Saskia cried and cried. When it seemed like she was out of tears, she wiped her red face, pushed out of my hug and sank down to the ground. She tucked her knees up into her chest and stared blankly at the opposite wall.

Grace, Zoe and I crowded in around her and sat at her feet. I put a comforting hand on her knee.

"How did you know I would be here?" Saskia finally asked, after a long period of silence.

"Ella worked it out," Zoe whispered.

Saskia looked at me. Her face, which was usually so confident and bright, looked timid and frightened.

"I knew about the missing key to the cabinet. And then when I heard it was being fixed tomorrow . . . well . . . I just figured it out," I mumbled. I didn't feel so clever anymore.

Saskia nodded. "Smart."

"Why did you do it?" Grace asked, gathering the spilled pages back into the folder and handing it to Saskia. "What's so important that it's worth risking expulsion for?"

Saskia looked at each one of us, then shrugged. She may as well come clean. "I stole the first items from other people, so that everyone would be focused on that. Nobody would notice a lost key if they were looking for other, more important things. And that meant I could steal the key and get access to the filing cabinet . . . which contained this." She opened the manila folder and held up some of the papers inside.

My eyes scanned over the pages, which had math and English questions all over them. At the top of one page the words "Streaming Test" jumped out like wild accusations.

"Are these our class tests?" Zoe asked.

Saskia nodded. "I've studied them. I know what the questions are, so I've already prepared the answers. I just wanted to be in the top stream, like my sister is," she trailed off.

"Saskia, you would have been in the top classes anyway!" I scolded. "Why risk expulsion? You could have done this on your own!"

"How do you know, Ella?" she said, slamming the fistful of pages down angrily. "In primary school I always had a tutor helping me with test preparation and assignments. What if I can't do it here on my own? What if I'm not . . . not good enough?" Fresh tears filled her blue eyes.

I patted Saskia's knee. Maybe all that confidence she normally had was just an act. Maybe Saskia was just as scared as the rest of us. Scared about school. Scared about living up to the standard of her sister. Scared about fitting in.

Saskia sniffed and lightly pushed my hand off her knee.

"And I know what you are going to do with this information, Ella."

"What?" I asked, confused.

"Oh, don't play dumb. I know you are going to put this in your story for *Eden Press*. I know that's why Grace is here with her camera. You want to expose me to the whole school."

"But that's not—" I began.

A loud *bang* interrupted me. The door to Mrs. Sinclair's office swung open and there stood Mrs. Sinclair, Ms. Montgomery and the school security guard.

The four of us squealed in shock.

Then we looked at each other with wide eyes.

We were in big trouble.

Chapter 18

One week later.

"In the name of privacy, this reporter has chosen not to reveal the identity of the Eden Thief. But the paper is happy to report that the thief has seen the error of her ways, and all the stolen items have been returned to their rightful owners.

Even though the items were just 'stuff,' these things were valuable not because of their monetary worth (that means how much they cost), but because of their *sentimental* worth. We Eden Girls are strong.

But we are also living far from our homes. Some of us desperately miss our families. And while we are like a family to each other, there are some days where a piece of our real homes is what we need to feel connected. Maybe it's your nonna's necklace. Or your aunt's scarf. Or maybe it's something that reminds you of a special person who is no longer with us. But so long as these items bind you to the giver, you will always have a reminder of that person who holds a special place in your heart. And that special bond is something that can never be stolen."

I finished reading my opinion piece and looked up nervously. The rest of the *Eden Press* team were silent. Ivy stood up and wiped a tear from her eye.

"Ella, that was beautiful," she sniffed. "That's exactly the kind of human-interest spin that we need in all our pieces. I think the school community is going to love the angle you've taken here!"

The other girls around the table began to applaud. My cheeks went bright red.

I looked to the end of the table and Saskia was

staring straight at me. Then she lifted her hands and began to join in with the clapping.

"I think it's going to be a unanimous decision here," Ivy said. "Ella, would you like to be the Junior Journalist for *Eden Press*? This means you'd get the main feature pieces covering your year group and you'd lead the other Year 7 girls in what you want them to write each month."

I nodded enthusiastically. "I'd love to!"

The end of lunchtime bell sounded and everyone hustled their belongings together. We all shuffled out of the meeting room and into the sunny day.

As I walked along, I breathed in the deep scent of jasmine on the wind. Above me, a kookaburra laughed gleefully. I smiled in agreement.

"Ella! Wait up!" a voice called from behind me. Saskia trotted up.

"Hi, Saskia."

"Ella, I just wanted . . . to say thank you."

"For what?"

"For not writing about me in your newspaper piece.

Thank you for not telling everyone—especially my sister—that I was the Eden Thief."

I nodded lightly. "I wouldn't do that to you, Saskia."

"I probably deserved it," she said quietly.

"Did you get into a lot of trouble?" I asked.

"Well, yes and no," she frowned. "Mrs. Sinclair did call my parents and we ended up having a video meeting with them, Ms. Montgomery and me. I finally told them about the pressure I was feeling to live up to Ivy. They'd never heard me talk about that before, so they were surprised. And they turned out to be pretty sympathetic. They said they would stop expecting me to be like my sister, as long as I promised to always try my best."

I smiled. "Sounds like a good compromise."

"Well," she added, "I am still grounded—no weekend passes or common room fun for four weeks— and, as part of my punishment, I have to help with kitchen duty for the rest of the term! It could have been a lot worse though, I suppose. You and Grace and Zoe didn't get in too much trouble, did you?"

"Nah, it was fine. Mrs. Sinclair understood why we did what we did. Thanks for backing us up as to why we were there. If you hadn't come clean, Mrs. Sinclair may have blamed us, too."

Saskia nodded slightly.

"But Ms. Montgomery made us write out the house rule about not sneaking out after dark, like, a thousand times, just to make sure we knew how to behave in the future." I grimaced.

Saskia grinned.

"I heard you got into the top stream after the tests," she said. "Congratulations."

"Thanks," I replied. "It really wasn't as big a deal as we were all making it out to be. I talked to Mrs. Sinclair about it, and she said I didn't need to worry about my scholarship. She told me just to do my best and that was always going to be enough."

The truth was, Mrs. Sinclair also told me that there were lots of girls on scholarships or other kinds of funded positions at the school. She said we make up a really important part of the school community, and I should never feel like I'm at risk of being sent away just because I'm on a scholarship. But I didn't tell that to Saskia.

"Well, you're going to have to put up with me in your classes, I'm afraid," Saskia said, smiling. "Mrs. Sinclair let me take a different test—one I hadn't seen before—and turns out I *can* get good marks just by using my brain! Who knew? So I'll be in the same stream as you. You'd better watch out!"

I wrinkled my nose up. Had Saskia really changed? She seemed pretty sorry. But there was always going to be that competitive streak to her, that's for sure. I knew I would have to keep my eyes open with her around. But at least we were heading in the right direction this time.

Saskia let out a little laugh and flicked her ponytail behind her as she skipped off up the path. I shook my head and smiled as I walked away to my next class.

Chapter 19

After classes the next day, I strolled down the path to the sick bay. The school nurse wanted to have a quick check of my eye to make sure everything still looked OK, after that dodgeball incident.

I walked up the steps and opened the glass-paneled door, which tinkled a little bell.

There, in the waiting area, sat Violet. She looked up at me with her big, round eyes behind her big, round glasses. She looked a little pale. I sat down next to her.

"How's it going?" I asked.

"Oh, Ella! It's fine. I'm fine. I mean, everything's fine."

I nodded.

Violet looked down at her hands.

I bit my lip gently and thought. Nanna Kate always says that some people wear their hearts on their sleeves. And other people shove them down deep into their pockets. I had a suspicion that Violet might be a heart-in-the-pocket kind of a girl. But that didn't mean she didn't need a friend.

"Violet, can I ask you something?" I said.

"Sure," she replied uncertainly.

"Are you OK?"

"What do you mean?"

"I mean, are you OK? I feel like we've all tried really hard to include you, but you don't want to hang out with us. And I have something to confess," I said slowly. I wasn't completely sure if I should admit what I was about to say. "We were trying to catch the Eden Thief, and we accidentally spied on you sneaking out late at night. And I know you sometimes disappear in the morning, too. And you always seem to hide away at dinner. What's going on?"

Violet's eyes searched the room desperately. I could see her mind was spinning, trying to think of what to say next. Eventually her shoulders slumped and she let out a long breath.

"I have diabetes," she blurted.

"Oh. Is that, like, because you ate too much sugar or something?"

"No!" Violet exploded.

I jumped back in alarm. I'd never heard Violet snap like that.

She composed herself, then continued in a calm voice. "Sorry. I mean, no. I have Type 1 diabetes. I was diagnosed at the age of one. It wasn't caused by a poor diet—it's a disease where my body has problems with insulin. Every day can feel like a battle. I have to monitor every single thing I eat. Every time I put something in my mouth, I have to calculate how much insulin I need in relation to that food. I can't just grab a snack and run off. It's just really . . . really hard, Ella." Her voice broke a little at the end.

I thought for a moment. "Surely there's only one

thing harder than what you're already doing . . ."

"Yeah, like what?" she asked.

"Dealing with everything you have to deal with AND trying to hide it at the same time," I said gently.

Violet sighed. "You're probably right, Ella. But I don't want to look like a freak. That's why I eat alone. I don't want people seeing that my meals are different. That's why I skipped the midnight feast—I can't just binge on candy whenever I choose. And that's why I seem to disappear all the time—I've been spending a lot of time down here with the nurse. If my blood sugar levels get too high or too low, I have to come down here for monitoring. The school is just getting used to managing my condition. They are being super careful with me and making sure I'm OK. Which is really great, but also really awkward. It's hard to make friends when you feel so different."

"It's also hard to make friends if you feel you can't be honest." My voice trailed off.

Violet and I sat in silence.

The nurse came out of the back room holding

186

something in her hand.

"Right, Violet, let's check your levels. Oh, Ella, hi," she said. "I'll just take Violet into the other room."

"Actually, if Ella doesn't mind, is it OK if we do it here?" Violet asked. "Only if it doesn't make you squeamish," she added to me.

"It's fine with me—I'd love to see how it works," I said, smiling.

Violet's concerned frown melted away and a bright smile spread across her face.

She took the tiny machine from the nurse.

"OK, Ella, it works like this."

After I left Violet to finish up with the nurse, I walked across the sweeping green grass of the manicured Centenary Lawn. I'd only been an Eden Girl for a few weeks, but I already felt like I knew the place inside out.

Nanna Kate says "home is where your heart is." The truth is, my heart will always be with my family. But as

I walked along that warm afternoon, breathing in the metallic scent of an impending summer storm, I felt like a piece of my heart was here with my Eden family, too. I thought of Grace. Of Zoe. Of Violet. Of our dorm room and our midnight feasts. And I wondered if, perhaps, one day, this really would be the place I called home.

Chapter 20

From: <u>Ella</u>

Sent: Saturday, 1:45 PM

To: <u>Olivia</u>

Subject: The Eden Ghost

Hi Olivia,

Everything is back to normal now that the whole Eden Thief thing is over. You have to promise you won't ever tell anyone it was Saskia, OK? Especially if you end up coming here one day. It's our secret, right?

Things are heaps better with Violet now, too. She told

Zoe and Grace about her diabetes as well, so now our whole room knows about it. She's heaps more relaxed about sharing with us and she's even started sitting with us at dinner. And Ms. Montgomery said that each one of us can take turns at being her buddy and making sure she isn't in need of any medical help. I'm actually really happy about that—I want to be able to help her. And, it turns out, she's actually really funny! I'd never seen her funny side before.

And guess what? Your ghost trap idea totally worked!!! Thanks for the suggestion to put flour on the floor outside our door, right before bedtime. You're right—if it was a ghost there would be no footprints, even if we heard the clinking sound. But there WERE footprints. Actually, not footprints, but PAW PRINTS! Turns out, Ms. Montgomery has a cat! The cat is always outside during the day, so I'd never seen her before, but at night she comes inside. And around her neck is a collar with two shiny, little crystals because the cat's name is Crystal! Whenever Crystal walks around, her collar makes a clinking sound.

So there's no ghost after all!

I'm pretty relieved actually. I didn't really want to live in a dorm with a ghost.

Anyway, I can hear Zoe calling. We are about to go for a walk with some Senior girls to the café in town for hot chocolate. It's one of our weekend privileges.

Email me soon.

I miss you, Olivia.

Love, Ella

xx

ELLA AT EDEN

Read all the Ella at Eden adventures:

New Girl
The Secret Journal